"Where Is This Former Fiancé?"

Jake's crisp voice galvanized her into action.

"Downstairs. He's coming up in a few minutes."

"Do you really want to get rid of him?" Jake was moving around the room with swift, economical movements. He removed his jacket and tie and rumpled his smoothly brushed hair. "Don't worry, you won't have to say a thing if you don't want to."

"I don't want a scene," she said uncertainly.

"If he has any sense, there won't be one," he assured her. "You wouldn't like to take off your dress, would you?"

RITA RAINVILLE
grew up reading truckloads of romances and replotting the endings of sad movies. She has always wanted to write the kind of romances she likes to read. She finds people endlessly interesting, and that is reflected in her writing. She is happily married and lives in California with her family.

Dear Reader:

I'd like to take this opportunity to thank you for all your support and encouragement of Silhouette Romances.

Many of you write in regularly, telling us what you like best about Silhouette, which authors are your favorites. This is a tremendous help to us as we strive to publish the best contemporary romances possible.

All the romances from Silhouette Books are for you, so enjoy this book and the many stories to come.

Karen Solem
Editor-in-Chief
Silhouette Books

RITA RAINVILLE
McCade's Woman

Silhouette Romance

Published by Silhouette Books New York

America's Publisher of Contemporary Romance

Silhouette Books by Rita Rainville

Challenge the Devil (ROM #313)
McCade's Woman (ROM #346)

SILHOUETTE BOOKS
300 E. 42nd St., New York, N.Y. 10017

Copyright © 1985 by Rita Rainville

Distributed by Pocket Books

ISBN: 0-373-08346-7

First Silhouette Books printing March, 1985

10 9 8 7 6 5 4 3 2 1

Map by Ray Lundgren

America's Publisher of Contemporary Romance

Printed in the U.S.A.

To Janice Lawrence and Jo Marshall,
a terrific support team

McCade's
Woman

SOUTHWEST
UNITED STATES

Places in _italics_ are fictitious.

Chapter One

"When's your friend coming, J.B.?"

"Pretty soon. She thought she'd be here early this afternoon."

The two deep voices carried clearly down the stairs and through the door of the entry room where Shanda St. James was waiting. One, mellowed by age, had a smooth cadence and a deliberate way of spacing words. Not quite a drawl, Shanda decided, just a certain softness in the vowel sounds. It was a sound she had listened to with increasing pleasure since crossing the Red River and entering Oklahoma earlier that morning.

"*She?* I thought it was one of your old oil field cronies who was coming."

Now *that* voice, Shanda thought with a frown, was an entirely different story. Sharp and incisive, it was about as friendly as a trained Doberman watching a nocturnal visitor crawl over a fence into its territory.

"Don't know how you came up with that idea, Jake,'' the older man commented mildly. "*I* didn't say so."

"Who is she, J.B.?" The tone of mounting irritation drew Shanda to the shadowy doorway. She watched in fascination as four pointed-toed leather boots, the cost of which could probably keep her new red Corvette in tires for the rest of its life, descended into view.

"A cousin." After an ominous pause, the older man continued. "At least I think that's what she is. I haven't figured it out yet, but she's going to stay with us for a while. She can probably explain it."

"I'll just bet she can. Damn it, J.B., I can't believe you've fallen for this phony relative routine again. Why don't you just let me handle her when she shows up?"

At home, which was Southern California—Los Angeles and Malibu to be exact—Shanda was known for her cool composure. Those who had witnessed her in a rage were grateful that they had not been the hapless target of her icy blue eyes and icier tone. Her last thought, before she stepped out of the room to enter the fray, was that it was a good thing she had had the foresight to confirm her hotel reservation before keeping this appointment.

The two wrangling male voices drowned out the click of Shanda's heels on the gleaming, black-and-white marble floor. As a result, when she stepped around the curve of the stairway, the two men drew to a startled halt as if the devil himself had reared up before them.

"Gentlemen." Her voice was barely more than a husky whisper as she swept them with a cursory glance. Both stood an inch or two over six feet. One was deeply bronzed, with black, Indian-straight hair and equally dark eyes. The other had bright blue eyes with a quizzical gleam in them and a shock of white hair. "You seem to be laboring under a couple of misapprehensions."

She looked directly at the dark one, who was several steps above her. "First of all, I do not need handling. In fact, I would object strenuously to it. Second, the relationship *is* valid. However, in the past, we were unaware of it and managed quite well; in the future, I think we may happily ignore it." Her eyes were contemptuous slits of blue as she slowly surveyed him from shiny boots to dark hair. "I neither need nor want your money . . . or anything else you might possess." She dismissed him with a blink of long, dark brown lashes.

She turned her attention next to the white-haired man. "I thank you for your gracious invitation to stay in your home, but you've overlooked the fact that I did not accept." A thread of regret slipped through her taut control. "We would have enjoyed talking, I think."

She wheeled around, heading for the door. With her hand on the knob, she turned for a final salvo. "Goodbye, gentlemen. It's been . . . interesting." As she gently closed the door behind her, she heard a muttered oath and a gust of pent-up air that sounded like an awed "Whooee!" She had no trouble guessing which came from whom!

Her long legs flew as she sprinted for the car. If she had correctly gauged the expression in those dark eyes, she didn't have time to dally. Smoothly, she buckled the seatbelt and turned the key in the ignition. The car murmured softly to life as the solid oak door of the imposing brick house was pulled open.

"Here he comes," she muttered aloud. "John Wayne charging down the trail to wallop the bad guy." She released the emergency brake, watching him rapidly cover the distance between them. Easing a slim foot down on the gas pedal, Shanda smiled mockingly and waggled her fingers in farewell as she slid away. The car snarled impolitely as it left him behind, his hands bunched on his slim hips, frozen in a wide-legged stance. Shanda could only assume that his moving lips were forming colorful phrases that would have added considerably to her already vivid vocabulary.

"And for that little contretemps," she murmured to herself as she wound along several broad, sycamore-shaded avenues, "I thank you very much, Aunt Paige." She turned onto Pennsylvania Avenue, left Nichols Hills behind, and headed south into the heart of Oklahoma City. Driving automatically, she thought about her aunt, a grandaunt, to be precise—her maternal grandfather's sister.

Shanda smiled as she recalled her aunt's laughing request. "Go to Oklahoma and bring me back a scoundrel!" Not a live one, to be sure; Aunt Paige's interest was in the past.

After retiring as a history professor at a small private college, she had turned her energy to genealogy, a hobby she had enjoyed for a number of years. Her business stationery now carried the initials C.A.L.S., Certified American Lineage Specialist, after her name. She and her staff enjoyed an impeccable reputation as professional genealogists. Her business gave her a legal and creative outlet for her curiosity and determination, she told Shanda with a youthful grin.

For years, in her spare time, she had been corresponding with far-flung relatives, following clues with the genteel persistence of Hercule Poirot, as she traced the family line of McCade. She also ruthlessly enlisted the aid of any able-bodied relative who had the good or bad fortune (depending upon their outlook) to cross her path. Thus, Shanda's involvement.

"Your mother is a McCade." Paige had stated the obvious a year ago, watching Shanda expectantly. "It's your moral obligation to learn about your past, to leave a legacy for the future, if you will."

"Aunt Paige, do you really think the coming generations are going to be all that thrilled about the bootleggers and horse thieves you've already dredged up?"

"Only one horse thief! Anyway, a black sheep or two makes better reading than any number of philanthropists and upright citizens." As many genealogists had before her, Paige planned to write an account of the McCade family, call it *Scoundrels and Scalawags* and distribute it to her increasingly apprehensive family members. A most appropriate title, Shanda thought as she blended in with the heavier traffic. An abundance of both had been ferreted out by her indefatigable aunt, along with a couple of skeletons that, in Shanda's opinion, would have better remained hidden in their cobwebby closets.

Reluctantly, but with increasing interest, Shanda had been drawn into her aunt's endless search. She had spent more hours than she cared to count at the Mission Viejo branch of the National Archives and the large genealogical libraries of the Mormon churches, muttering maledictions at ink-stained pages and the fanciful spelling of the family names as interpreted by the census takers of yore.

Parking her car in the hotel lot, she took the elevator to her room and dropped down onto the queen-size bed.

Aunt Paige would not be pleased, Shanda decided, staring reflectively at the ceiling. She further decided that Aunt Paige, though lively and lovable, was becoming a pain in the neck. She had already unearthed facts that might well be embarrassing to some, decidedly awkward for others. And with an historian's disregard for anything other than the truth, Paige planned to print it all. And now she expected Shanda to help with her latest project.

Even if Shanda were so inclined, helping would not be a simple matter. Her encounter at the McCade house had made that clear. The older man had the look of one who had fought his battles, passed on the title and was now content to watch the arena from the observer's post, offering infrequent but pungent advice.

But the other one—the problem would be with him. Of necessity, Shanda had learned to size up people quickly and she trusted her instincts. What she didn't trust was *him*. His dark eyes had not blinked as he had leisurely surveyed her—although, she admitted with a surge of feminine satisfaction, they *had* widened, resting briefly on the curve of her breasts before dropping to her small waist and round hips. Her mauve silk dress might have been nonexistent for all the protection it offered from his scrutiny. Any woman would recognize him for what he was. Trouble with a capital T. And having just ended an engagement with one maddening male, she was less than thrilled to find another one in her path.

She punched a pillow and thrust it under her head, deliberately erasing men from her mind. Instead, she remembered how excited her aunt had been when she had called last month. "Shanda! I've just found out what happened to Buell!"

Shanda had mentally sifted through family and mutual acquaintances. "What's that?" she'd murmured, hoping she could bluff her way through. Aunt Paige tended to be hurt if one lost track of her cast of characters.

"Well, he died, of course," Paige said calmly.

"Good heavens! When?"

"About fifty years ago."

"I should have known," Shanda muttered in amused exasperation. "All right, which relative have you exhumed now?"

"My grandfather, of course. Your great-great grandfather. I told you all about him last month," Paige reminded her.

"I was busy winding up my film and I guess it didn't sink in. You'd better run through it again." Ignoring her aunt's exaggerated sigh, she listened carefully.

"I always believed my grandfather Buell died long before I was born," Paige had said. "Everyone thought so. No one ever talked about him, and all anyone could remember about my grandmother was that she lived with her oldest son and sat all day in a rocking chair smoking a corncob pipe."

"A *what?* You didn't tell me about them," Shanda had stated positively. "I would have remembered that."

"So," Paige had continued ruthlessly, "we all figured that Grandpa was dead."

"And Grandma found solace in a rocking chair and pipe. Terrific."

"But I've never been able to find a record of his death," Paige persevered, oblivious of Shanda's flippancy. "Until today. Someone answered a query that I placed in a genealogy newsletter. They even sent me a copy of his obituary!'' If Paige had received a letter awarding her the mineral rights to the Tulsa oil fields, she wouldn't have been more excited.

"I feel as though I've missed the point somewhere along the way," Shanda had complained.

"Don't you see? He didn't die when everyone thought he did. He just disappeared. Not only did he go away, he married a younger woman and started another family.'' Paige was mumbling to herself, obviously reading the lengthy newspaper article. "Why the old goat! He was sixty-eight and he married a woman of twenty-six! Can you believe that? He died when he was eighty-eight."

Shanda had grinned. She could imagine the narrow brows forming white arches of disdain as her aunt clicked her tongue in disapproval.

"Why his son, J.B., if he's still alive, would be just my age! But what's even worse, Grandma was still alive when he married that other woman.''

"Well," Shanda had said reasonably, "if I were married to a woman who sat in a rocker, muttering and sucking on a pipe, I'd run away with someone else, too. Preferably a young and pretty someone."

"Hmm." Paige had been abstracted, obviously still scanning the material before her. "It doesn't say anything about a divorce.''

Shanda had snapped to attention. She knew that speculative tone. Paige was already sifting through the information looking for items of interest for the family saga. Unfortunately, in this case, it could be bigamy, compounded by illegitimacy. "That doesn't mean they weren't divorced," she had cautioned. "After all, you couldn't find his death certificate, but he was dead.''

Later, Shanda had tried to convince her tiresome aunt to

investigate some other branch of the family. It was a stalwart attempt, but doomed from the start. She would have made more luck diverting an avalanche.

Paige had already made her plane reservations. She was determined to learn about her grandfather's second family, and if she found that wife number two was acquired without a divorce from number one, so much the better. It would make a fascinating chapter, didn't Shanda agree?

Two days before Paige was to leave, Shanda's telephone had rung. It was an ordinary ring, certainly not one to warn her that she had suddenly been deserted by her guardian angel.

"Hello."

"Shanda! Thank God you're home!"

"What's the matter, Aunt Paige? You sound upset."

"Upset? *Upset*. I'm more than that. I'm frantic. Do you know what that murderous little terror who lives next door did to me?"

"That brown-eyed kid who melts you with a glance— what's his name?—Tony? You know you adore him."

"Hah! If I ever get my foot back on the ground, I just might use it on his backside."

Shanda had stared at the telephone in puzzlement. "Aunt Paige," she had asked carefully, "just where is your foot now?"

"God give me patience, girl. It's on the end of my leg in the air!"

Grateful that the other woman could not see the grin on her face, Shanda had subdued the quiver of amusement in her voice. "Let me guess. You've taken up can-can dancing and froze in a high kick."

"Very funny."

"How many more guesses do I get?"

"None. The little wretch ran me down with his skateboard and I'm flat on my back in a disgusting plaster cast with my leg attached to a pulley."

"*What?* You should have called me."

"I *am* calling you," was the testy reply. "Shanda," her voice had changed abruptly, "you have to go to Oklahoma for me."

"*Me?* Aunt Paige, I don't have the training to get the kind of information you need. Anyone on your staff would do a better job."

"You're an historian. You certainly know how to dig for information. Besides, I want this done by someone in the family and since I'm chained to this contraption, that leaves you."

Ignoring the bulldog determination in Paige's voice, Shanda had reasoned gently. "You know you want to meet them. J.B. will still be there when your leg heals."

"Maybe. But men that age sometimes just keel over with no warning."

"But I thought you said he was about your age."

There was a long pause and then a deep sigh. "Shanda, I know I've led you to believe otherwise, but seventy is not the first flush of youth. I don't want J.B. turning up his toes before he tells us about his father."

"But—"

"Remember the work I was doing for the Finley family? I found that aunt who had material on three generations. But before I got to her, she stepped on a roller skate—probably left on the sidewalk by the kid next door—landed on her head and took all the information with her. *Three* generations.

"J.B. could have that much or more and I won't take a

chance on him slipping through my fingers. He could have a bad heart. He might lose his memory or—''

"All right, Aunt Paige. All *right*.''

So Shanda eventually found herself agreeing that, yes, she was off for two months. And yes, she was planning a long trip through the southwestern states. Yes, she supposed she could stop in Oklahoma City and meet the "other" family. But that wasn't all she would do, Shanda promised herself. She would personally search all the divorce records in the state of Oklahoma until she found one for the elderly but active Buell.

With that in mind, Shanda wrote a polite letter to J.B. McCade introducing herself, briefly explained the relationship and asked to meet with him at some convenient time. By return mail, she had received a note from J.B. saying that he and his son, Jake, would like her to be their guest for as long as she planned to be in the area. Overwhelmed by such graciousness, but not wishing to take advantage of the warmly offered Southern hospitality, Shanda had gently refused, but had given the date she expected to arrive and asked if she could stop by early in the afternoon.

Enough of the past. Shanda rose from the bed and walked to the closet. Right now, all she was interested in was taking a long bath, relaxing for a while and then having dinner.

Four hours later, she stood at the door of the chandeliered dining room. Her luxuriant mass of chestnut hair had been disciplined into a soft, half-braided coil. The severe style, while harsh for some, only served to emphasize her wide-set eyes and the pure line of her oval face. At the age of fourteen, when she had reluctantly conceded that she would never be the diminutive redhead of her dreams, she had, in a typically thorough manner, set about making the most of her excellent bone structure.

Although her escorts issued lavish compliments, she remained more objective. Balancing a too-generous mouth against a too-small nose, she evaluated her appearance as somewhere between interesting and intelligent, with the scale sliding toward the latter.

She stood quietly as the maître d' approached. Her dress was a sleeveless cloud of lilac georgette, with a sheer ruffle falling from the round neckline and lightly covering her upper arms. A pink cummerbund molded the waist and fell softly to her knees.

"Is madame waiting for someone?"

"No, madame is alone," she replied serenely.

"A pity."

Shanda grinned, first at his involuntary comment, then at his appalled expression. "Yes, isn't it?" She followed his stiffly erect back to a corner table with an excellent view of the room.

A few minutes later, sipping an excellent Chardonnay, she looked up from a leisurely inspection of the menu. And almost choked. Bearing down on her with the expression of one determined to make amends for a lamentable faux pas, the maitre d' was escorting a man to her table.

The wine turned to vinegar on her tongue as she looked up into dark eyes daring her to object.

Chapter Two

"Good evening," bit off the never-to-be-forgotten voice above her as she controlled her expression. She nodded distantly as he drew out the chair across from her and sat down.

"Did you remember a few more insults you wanted to hurl at me?" she asked once the waiter was out of earshot.

His words were as abrupt as his tone. "I had a hell of a time finding you."

"I didn't expect you to look." She marveled at his nerve. He was actually complaining that she hadn't made things more convenient for him!

"Really?"

"If you *didn't* come to insult me, I should warn you that you're coming perilously close."

She sat silently, studying the rugged, closed face. His eyes were no more revealing than they had been earlier.

Obviously he had learned early in life to keep his own counsel. Other lessons had followed, taking their toll in trust and innocence. He was thirty-four or five and looked every year of it. Creases were etched at the corners of his eyes, and she would bet her current contract that they weren't smile lines. No, she decided, amusement would rarely brighten the ebony glitter of those eyes.

He looked up from the menu, meeting her gaze. "Do you know what you want?" At her nod he took charge, signaled the hovering waiter with a glance and ordered their meal. When they were alone, he leaned back, a dark brow slowly arching. "Get it off your chest," he invited, "before you explode."

She frowned, mistrusting this large, suddenly bland man. She knew that he was hard and uncompromising, and yet he sat there in his perfectly tailored evening clothes looking as if he had nothing more on his mind than enjoying his steak and her company. What was he up to?

"I don't believe in coincidence, Jake McCade. Just what brings you to this particular place tonight?"

"You."

"I'm flattered."

"I wanted to see what you looked like when you weren't madder than hell and shooting icicles from your eyes."

"If that's all you intended, you could have peeked over the waiter's shoulder and left. No need to commit yourself to a dinner."

"And the evening," he added.

"Dinner," she amended.

"What are *you* doing here, Shanda St. James?"

She didn't pretend to misunderstand him. "Have you asked your father?"

"Yes. But he was a bit . . . touchy after you left. He said if I wanted to know, to come and ask you."

"It's very simple," she said, resisting the impulse to be difficult. "I have an aunt who is a genealogist. She discovered that we all share a common ancestor and suggested that I make a courtesy call on my way through the state."

"Exactly how are we related?" he interrupted.

"Damned if I know." She grinned at his sudden frown. "But if Aunt Paige is right, J.B. is—wait a minute, don't rush me—my half-great-granduncle. And you are my half-first cousin, twice removed," she finished triumphantly.

"You are no relative of mine." The words were deliberately spaced, uttered with absolute certainty.

"What makes you say that?"

"One reason, which we'll discuss later. And one very basic instinct." He grinned broadly, his eyes lighting with an unholy amusement. "I've never yet met a cousin that I wanted to toss over my shoulder and haul to the nearest bed. We'll talk about that later, too," he assured her. "Right now, finish your story."

She stared wide-eyed, wondering if she were losing her mind. These last few months *had* been hectic and breaking up with Lee hadn't helped. Shaking her head once, as if that small act could restore her control, she plodded on. After briefly describing the information that had recently come into her aunt's possession, but omitting Paige's speculations and expectations, Shanda concluded with, "So Aunt Paige was hoping that J.B. could tell me something about his father."

"Is that all?" The words were neutral, but Shanda felt his disbelief.

"No."

The waiter appeared at that moment with their salads and hot rolls. Shanda beamed a brilliant smile at him, detaining him for a few moments while Jake's black eyes bored into her.

"Thank you." The deep, cold voice had the dual effect of stopping Shanda's stream of pleasantries in midsyllable and of making the waiter disappear. "You were saying?" Jake asked her.

"Nothing important," she said innocently. "I was just telling the waiter that the rolls smelled delicious." She leaned back like a satisfied cat as the dark eyes glittered with restrained ire.

"You know damned well what I'm talking about. What else does your aunt want?"

"Oh, that," she said just before taking a bite of her salad. She chewed it long enough to gain the approval of the dental association and to glimpse another flicker of temper in the watchful eyes. It's almost like taking candy from a baby, she thought in contentment as she carefully replaced her fork. "If J.B. proved to be approachable," she said slowly, dragging it out as long as possible, "I was to ask if he had any photos of his father. And if he did, I was to ask permission to have a few copies made."

"That's it?" he asked blankly.

"That's it." The words were crisp.

"It doesn't make sense," he said finally. They had finished their salads in silence and he was swiftly disposing of a very rare steak.

"It makes all the sense in the world if you're on the trail of a lost ancestor. Obviously, you've never known anyone who's tracing a family genealogy. It becomes an obsession. It's a bit like panning for gold. Each new clue or contact is a shiny nugget. You've hit pay dirt if you find someone who knew your ancestor. If they have pictures, you've found the mother lode."

She could sense the sharply rising suspicion in him as he examined her face. Exasperation vied with amusement within her until an entirely unexpected emotion replaced them both. How odd. The last thing she expected to feel for this self-assured and rather overwhelming man was sympathy. Obviously, because of some hard-learned lessons, he couldn't accept the simple truth for what it was. Of course, if she were another type of person, he might well have something to worry about.

"It's a good story," he said finally. "Too bad I don't believe it."

So much for sympathy. She was not accustomed to having her word doubted. She didn't like it. Not one little bit.

"Then it's a good thing I came to see your father, isn't it?" she answered with a touch of asperity.

"You'll be dealing with me soon enough if you're here for any of the usual reasons."

"And they are?"

"A con game, blackmail, or some publicity stunt."

"Good grief, it sounds like you spend your days fending off pretenders to the throne."

"It's not a full-time job, but it keeps me busy enough. J.B.'s a lot more trusting than I am."

She made one last attempt. After all, the man *was* concerned about his father, even if he was rude and obnoxious. Her eyes shone with honesty as she faced him across the table. "Jake, I'm here for one reason. I just want J.B. to tell me what he remembers about his father. It's as simple as that. I promise you that I won't presume upon his good will.''

His hard face didn't soften; she drew a deep breath and forged on. ''You can see''—she gestured lightly with one hand, indicating the room—''that I like nice things. But I pay my own bills and I can afford to do so. As I said earlier, I don't need the McCade money.''

She might have saved her breath for all the acknowledgment she received. His next words startled her.

''J.B. wants to see you.''

''Fine. I'll call him and make arrangements.''

''Tonight. At the house.''

''No.''

''What the hell do you mean, no?''

''I tried it once, remember? I won't put myself in that position again.''

''Obviously, you don't subscribe to the philosophy of forgiving and forgetting.''

''I have a very long memory. Besides, no one has offered me an apology.''

''Oh.'' It was an irritated grunt. ''I was getting around to that. I just wanted to explain a few things first.''

''Don't bother,'' she said drily. ''You get top marks for exposition, but you just flunked repentance.''

They both declined dessert but opted for more coffee. She remembered something he had said earlier. ''Jake, what did you mean about using J.B. for publicity?''

''For years now, every time there's been a free inch of space in a newspaper or magazine, someone has wanted to do an article on old oil money, the ten wealthiest families in the state or some other damn fool thing. Lately it's been

TV people wanting to do in-depth interviews. You wouldn't believe some of the approaches they use. If it weren't for the patrol cars in our area, we'd probably have a camera unit camping in our front yard.''

"Are you *that* rich?'' she asked in an odd voice.

"Yes.''

She didn't doubt him. Accustomed as she was to the hyperbole of the Hollywood scene, the terse monosyllable was more convincing than any number of superlatives.

"Why the aversion to publicity?'' she asked lightly. "Do you have skeletons tucked away in the back room?''

"Nothing so interesting.'' His grim expression lightened as he observed her look of amused curiosity. "We just don't like living our lives on center stage. In fact, we work hard at protecting our privacy so we can live a fairly normal life with the same anonymity that most people have.''

"I can understand that,'' she murmured with more feeling than she knew.

"So you'll come back to the house?'' he asked, sensing her softened mood even if he didn't understand the reason behind it.

She had to give him credit, Shanda thought. He didn't miss a trick. With such a keen ear for nuances, the inclination for swift action, and a superb sense of timing, it was no wonder that the family coffers were overflowing.

"No,'' she replied serenely, ignoring his scowl. "But I will call and ask if he'll be my guest for lunch or dinner.''

"We accept,'' he said promptly.

"*You* aren't invited,'' she pointed out. "I'm trying to get information, not waste my time dodging verbal bullets.''

"I'll be on my best behavior," he promised.

"I don't think you know the meaning of the word. No," she said definitely, "not this time."

Only a slight twitch at the corner of her mouth betrayed her amusement. Obviously, the wealthy Mr. McCade was not accustomed to being rejected. The startled flash in his eyes on an otherwise sternly controlled face bore mute testimony to the fact.

"No," she added for good measure, "you go take care of your oil wells. J.B. and I will do just fine."

She watched with interest as a muscle bunched in his jaw and his chin grew even more determined. "Has anyone ever told you that you need a good, strong hand to keep you in line?" he inquired with a rasp.

"Um hum." She nodded in affirmation. "Some have even tried to supply it."

"And?"

"It didn't work."

"Obviously, they didn't know how to apply it so that it would do the most good."

"And you would?"

"Yes." Once again the terse response was convincing.

"I'd like to see you try it!"

"Keep it up, honey, and you'll get a firsthand demonstration."

Deciding that a strategic withdrawal was in order, Shanda contented herself with a glare over her coffee cup. She ignored him as he signaled the waiter and watched in stony silence as he dropped several large bills on the small tray. She had intended to pay for her own meal, but since he was determined to be the man in charge, let him use a nice chunk of his money. Too bad she hadn't ordered something more expensive!

His hand was at the small of her back as she threaded her way through the tables to the large doorway. She stopped at the first elevator, bringing her persistent escort to a reluctant halt.

"It's still early. Are you sure you won't reconsider and come to the house?"

"Positive. I've had a long day and I'm ready to go to bed." She extended her hand and said briskly, "Thank you for the dinner."

He looked down at her slim fingers, unexpectedly laced them through his and turned to face the elevator. "I'll see you to your room."

"No!" The protest was instinctive, in response to a prickly warning that scampered down her spine. It wasn't that she was afraid, she assured herself, she just didn't want him anywhere near her room.

The ride up was too fast. Before she realized that he had completely ignored her objection, Shanda was staring in fascination at his large, outstretched hand. It was broad-palmed and tan, well-kept but slightly rough-textured. It was also demanding her key. A quick glance at his face convinced her that they would remain outside her door all night if she didn't produce it.

Fuming, she dug in her gold mesh evening purse and dropped the key into his hand. The door was unlocked and she was ushered into the small suite. He switched on a brass table lamp and disappeared into the dark bedroom without a word. Shanda leaned back against the wall, listening as he opened and closed doors. She wasn't going to budge, she decided. Give the man an inch and he'd be sitting down on the floral sofa, calling room service for drinks and settling down for the evening.

"I don't recall inviting you in," she observed as he strolled back into the lighted room.

"Someone had to do burglar patrol," he said easily, "and I'm better equipped for it than you are."

"Thank you very much," she began, obviously intending to hustle him out of the door, only to be interrupted by the muted purr of the telephone.

"Shall I?" He reached out until his hand hovered over the demanding instrument.

"No!" She pushed away from the wall, frowning impartially at him and the noisy intruder. "Hello." Her fierce expression faded, blossoming into a radiant smile. "Barry! I didn't expect to hear your voice for a month or so. Let me guess, you miss me already, right?" She turned her back to Jake, unaware that he moved so that he could watch her animated face in the wall mirror.

"Right, love," came the wry voice of her cameraman and best friend. "So do Nora and Todd. Ouch! Nora, grab that kid, his knees are drilling holes in me!" She heard Nora's snicker and Todd's bubbling, one-syllable chant as he crawled over his father's lanky, obviously recumbent form. Shanda grinned. They had been part of her life for some time now. She had worked with Nora and Barry at the studio, been in their wedding and was now proud godmother to their young hell raiser.

"By all means," she encouraged. "Take care of that manly form. I have plans for your bod for the next year or so."

A dark frown settled on Jake's face. Happily, she was unaware of the man stiffening as he stood behind her. "Nice as this is," she teased, "you must have some reason for calling besides informing me of your deteriorating physical condition."

"I wish you'd watch your tongue," Barry complained amiably. "Nora's right here beside me taking notes. Probably collecting future blackmail material."

"Well, I knew you before she did. I have a prior claim."

"Wrong, Shanda." Nora's voice was warm with contentment as she grabbed the receiver. "He's mine now. The only time you get him is when his hands are full of camera."

"I never thought she'd get so possessive, Barry," Shanda said in a mournful tone. "Well, if there's no other way out of it, we'll just have to share you." Shanda's good humor was not shared by her silent companion. He turned to an ice-filled bucket, withdrew a bottle of wine and opened it. Only a certain precision to his movements and the stiff set of his shoulders betrayed his anger.

"Don't give up so easily, love," Barry urged. "Can't have her getting too complacent. Besides, after living so long in a place crammed with male models, all equipped with muscles that jump on command, this is great for my ego!"

Shanda spun around as she heard the ring of glass on crystal, but she could see only Jake's broad back. Now, wanting to end the conversation before Jake made himself too much at home, she pressed, "What's up, Barry?"

"Well, aside from wanting to know that you arrived safely, I just called to remind you that if you see any interesting material, I've got some time to come down and shoot it."

"You told me that before I left," she reminded him.

"Yeah, I know. Uh, there is one more thing." He drew the words out reluctantly. "Lee's looking for you."

"What! Does—"

"Yeah, he knows where you are and I wouldn't be surprised if he shows up."

"How—"

"I'm afraid it's my fault. I thought you had told him your itinerary before you broke up, and I mentioned that you'd be settled there for a week or so. It wasn't until he walked away with that damned smirk that I realized I had told him exactly what he wanted to know. I just called to apologize and warn you."

Shanda watched Jake settle two wineglasses within reach, ease down on the sofa and cross booted feet on the coffee table. Boots with evening clothes? she wondered. "Thanks, Barry. I understand. And I appreciate the warning. It helps to be prepared," she murmured absently as she watched Jake sample the wine with appreciation. "Don't worry. I'll handle it."

"Shanda, you won't—"

This time she interrupted him. "No, I won't. I promise. It's over. Past history. See you in a month or so," she murmured softly before replacing the receiver.

"Where did you get that?" She pointed an accusing finger at the bottle of wine.

"Had it sent up while we were having dinner." He patted the cushion next to him. "Come and try it."

Exactly how stupid does he think I am? she wondered as she refused the wine and deliberately sat in a graceful, high-backed chair across from him. The coffee table made a nice, solid barrier, she decided. "I thought you wanted to get me to your house, so why this?" She gestured at the pale wine.

"It's what you call planning for contingencies. If you had gone, you'd have found it when you returned. Since you didn't, we have a chance to enjoy it and get to know each other.''

Coming from anyone else, it would have sounded matter-of-fact, a natural thing to say. From him, it had a decidedly ominous overtone.

''Sounds nice, but I don't buy it. What you really want to know is what devious plans I have in store for J.B. Right?''

''Wrong. What I really want to know,'' he continued deliberately, ''is when you'll go to bed with me.''

Well, he certainly couldn't be accused of equivocation, Shanda decided ruefully. Here was plain speaking with a vengeance! She cast him a look of active dislike, decided that she did, after all, need a calming sip of wine, and promptly choked. Even in the midst of her wheezing, nose-burning misery, she was aware that he moved with well-coordinated speed. He would, of course. He whacked her heartily on the back, scooped her out of the chair, returned to the sofa and dropped back down with her in his lap.

He examined her watery eyes, then nodded in approval as she drew in a ragged breath. Just as she was beginning to wiggle in protest, he further enraged her by commenting, ''You really shouldn't drink if you can't handle it.''

She leaned back against his supporting arm, missing the flash of satisfaction that crossed his face, and in a strangled whisper repeated, ''Can't *handle* . . . That had nothing to do with the wine and you know it! What I had trouble swallowing was your question.''

''Why? I'd have thought that living in a fast-lane city would have taught you how to cope with that.''

Shanda snorted in disgust. ''You've been reading those

movie tabloids, I see. Not everyone in Southern California spends their time bounding from one bed to another. There are a few people around who lead ordinary lives.''

''Does that mean you've never slept with a man?''

With an obvious effort, she restrained her temper. ''That is none of your business. I was,'' she explained loftily, ''speaking in general terms.''

''But I wasn't asking everyone in Southern California to share my bed. Just you.''

She scrambled off his lap and sat at the other end of the sofa, one knee folded under her, facing him. ''Well, I'm not interested. Besides, you're my cousin, for heaven's sake!''

''Come on, Shanda. I'm no more related to you than I am to J.B.'s coon cat.''

''His *what?*''

''Never mind.'' He sighed. ''I'm sorry I mentioned it.''

''You still don't believe me, do you?'' she asked, returning to the subject at hand.

''That has nothing to do with this. But even if we were cousins, the half-assed relationship you described would have no effect on us.'' He looked at her baffled expression and with all the aplomb of a magician removing a rabbit from his hat, he asked, ''Didn't your research bring out the fact that I'm adopted?''

Deliberately, she kept her face blank as she reevaluated her position. She had walked into this mess thinking she would be dealing with relatives. Distant, yes, but still family.

Now, with just a few words, the entire situation had changed, and handling it would be about as tricky as walking a tightrope with a bottle of nitroglycerin. She now

had on her hands a stubborn, determined, sexy-as-hell
man whose eyes were indicating that he didn't have a
familial bone in his muscular body. She had a gloomy
feeling that things were not going to improve in the
immediate future.

She was right. In the next several minutes, she was
forced to revise drastically her original estimation of him.
Not only did he come equipped with a sense of humor, but
it was a wicked one. And what was worse, it glimmered in
his eyes, deepened the creases in his lean cheeks and left
her feeling decidedly vulnerable. Men with smiling eyes
had become a rare commodity in her life.

"Adopted," he verified, nodding his head compla-
cently.

"You would be," she said bitterly.

He had the look of a man well satisfied as he shifted his
weight to face her. His arm stretched along the back
cushion, his fingers resting near her outstretched hand. "I
thought you'd be pleased."

"Why on earth should I be?"

"Well, with your fixation about this family thing, I
knew you wouldn't want to make love to a cousin," he
explained helpfully.

It took a moment for his words to sink in. Shanda sat
stupefied, staring. He was either the most egotistical
animal on two legs or the most persistent. Or both. She
took another look and saw that behind that good ole boy
smile there was a nasty intelligence at work. He was
analyzing her every reaction and storing it for future
reference.

"I have exactly the same reservations about strangers,"
she said.

"Too soon?"

"Definitely!"

"I'll wait. Tomorrow will be just fine."

"Look," she advised kindly, "why don't you forget that today ever happened. Call one of your women and just carry on as you were before I came along."

She watched something flicker deep within his eyes. Anger? she wondered. No, not that. Oddly enough, it was easier to tell what it *wasn't*. It wasn't passion, lust or even desire. But it was familiar. She cast about, trying to pinpoint where she had last encountered that look and almost groaned aloud. It was the exact expression that Aunt Paige had when she was on the trail of some juicy morsel and was not about to be sidetracked. It was a combination of hunting instinct and sheer slug-it-out-toe-to-toe determination. Aunt Paige she could cope with; she wasn't so sure about this one.

"That presents a problem." He touched her fingers with his own. "Because I want *you*."

"Sorry," she replied, not at all apologetically, "you can't have me."

"Why not?"

"Well, for starters, you insulted me before you even met me, then hunted me down to finish the job. You think that I'm a con artist, a potential blackmailer, and that I have evil designs on J.B."

The corners of his mouth lifted in a reluctant grin. "Besides that."

"Isn't that enough, for heaven's sake? All right!" she said crossly, yanking her hand away as his thumb smoothed the back of it. "I don't want a man in my life. I just got rid of one and I'm in no hurry to replace him."

"Who is he? The one on the phone?"

"No."

"Did you live with him?"

"No, but he thought I was going to. We were engaged," she added reluctantly as he waited, pinning her to the couch with his laser-beam stare.

"Why did you break it off?"

"How do you know I did?" she asked with interest.

"Because only a fool would walk away from you and you wouldn't be involved with a fool."

"Thank you." She was amazed at the rush of pleasure she felt at his words.

"So?"

She sighed in exasperation. Where did these people get the energy for such relentless interrogations? she wondered as she had so often before when Aunt Paige was in top form.

"He didn't really want to get married. Fortunately, I discovered that, and a few other things, before the situation got too complicated."

"I was wrong." Jake's voice had an oddly satisfied ring to it. "He *is* a fool. How'd he take being dumped?"

Her look was scathing. "You have such a charming way of expressing yourself. "Badly," she finally admitted. "He's not used to . . . being the dumpee."

"But it's over?"

"As far as I'm concerned."

"Ah."

She stiffened. "And exactly what does that mean?"

"Don't waste your bristle on me," he advised imperturbably. "It means that he's giving you a bad time and you could probably use some help."

"I'm doing just fine," she assured him. "All he needs

is a little time to get used to the idea." A little time and a lot of space, she thought. That wasn't asking too much, was it?

Apparently it was. The telephone buzzed for the second time that evening and, with a faint stirring of premonition, she reached for it.

"Shanda St. James."

"Hello, darling."

The warm baritone voice that kept women glued to their television sets every Monday evening at eight, palpitating with romantic longings, had just the opposite effect on Shanda.

"Hello, Lee," she said and watched with resignation as Jake's dark brows rose.

"Darling," the flexible voice was shaded with just the lightest touch of reproach, "why did you leave without telling me?"

"I didn't think it was necessary."

"Then you really meant it, didn't you?"

"Of course I did. Look, Lee," she persevered, ignoring Jake, who was listening with interest, "the fact that we look well together when we go out is not enough. There's more to life than being photogenic." She scowled at Jake as he grinned.

"What we need to do," Lee said confidently, "is talk about it."

Shanda groaned inwardly. They were right back to square one! "All right." She sighed. "When I get back to L.A. in about six weeks, if you still want to talk, we will. How's that?"

"How about six minutes?"

"What! What do you mean? Lee, where are you?" Prompted by the note of urgency in her voice, Jake unfolded his length and came to stand by her. If she hadn't long since passed the stage of stamping her feet and screeching in irritation, she would have done just that at Lee's response.

"Downstairs, darling. In the lobby. I'm checking in, but first," his voice lowered, "I have to do a little P.R. The desk clerk and a couple of women want my autograph."

"But, Lee—"

"Can't talk now, darling. See you in a few minutes."

Chapter Three

Shanda slowly replaced the receiver. "Damn it all to hell," she said in heartfelt exasperation.

"Where is he?" Jake's crisp voice galvanized her into action. Crossing the room, she shot the security bolt on the door and turned to face him.

"Downstairs. He's coming up in a few minutes." Catching his sardonic look at the bolted door, she said, "All right! So everything isn't as fine as I thought it was!"

"Did I say anything?"

"You don't have to. You have very speaking eyebrows."

"How much good do you think that's going to do?" he asked.

"It'll buy me some time."

"Why not just let him in and tell him to get lost?"

"Because he doesn't listen. And he's convinced that if

40

he talks long enough and loud enough, I'll change my mind. I've been through that scene twice and I'm not crazy about doing it a third time."

"Do you really want to get rid of him?"

"You don't listen either, do you? I'm not playing hard to get; I'm just too tired to go through it again. I don't want to talk to him right now."

"Just making sure." Jake was moving around the room with swift, economical movements. The ice bucket was placed on the coffee table near their wineglasses. He removed his jacket and tie and rumpled his smoothly brushed hair. "Don't worry, you won't have to say a thing if you don't want to."

He was very much the man in charge, Shanda noted in vexation as he unbolted the door and left it very slightly ajar. "I don't want a scene," she said uncertainly.

"If he has any sense, there won't be one," he assured her. "You wouldn't like to take off your dress, would you?"

"I would not," she snapped. "He doesn't have an awful lot, of sense that is."

"Too bad. About the dress," he explained as she looked at him in confusion. "It would have added a nice touch. As for the other, I guess I'll just have to do the thinking for all three of us. Do you have some deep-seated attachment to those shoes?" he asked before she could utter the hot words forming on her tongue.

"Shoes?" she repeated stupidly. The man leaped from one thing to another like a flea on a griddle! *Now* what was he talking about? She stared down at the offending sandals. Actually, they were just a few wispy gold straps and high heels. Very pretty, she thought.

"Would you mind taking them off?" he asked patiently.

"Is all this really necessary?" Shanda grumbled. She put a hand on Jake's arm to support herself while she slipped off first one, then the other. It was amazing, the difference three inches made. Her head was now level with his shoulders instead of that determined chin and suddenly she felt fragile, vulnerable. A strange feeling. She didn't think she liked it.

Jake nudged her shoes with the toe of his booted foot until they rested beside the couch. He undid several buttons of his shirt and ran a critical eye over her hair. "No, that won't do. You look too untouched," he said. "Turn around."

Shanda obediently turned her back to him. He released several pins and she felt the weight of her hair tumble to her shoulders. He turned her around and nodded approvingly. "That's better."

It had been no more than a minute since Shanda had hung up the telephone and in that time, she realized, he had taken over. And she had allowed him to do so. Why? She wished she knew. But she had the feeling that even if she had resisted, he would have ended up the same way—in charge. Definitely a man of action. It was a nice change, she decided, to let someone else handle everything. But the novelty would soon wear off, she reflected. She was not the type to put the running of her life into another's hands. At least, not for long.

And what about Jake? She would wager her next year's salary that he did nothing without a reason and, in this particular case, she had a very good idea of what it was. Yes, he would help her, but only to gain his own end. And this scenario he was setting up? Deliberately, she studied the pros and cons, then shrugged. It couldn't hurt, but it remained to be seen whether or not it would succeed. Lee Masters, she had learned during their brief engagement, believed his own publicity. It would take a touch of genius to convince him that Shanda could actually prefer another man.

Jake dropped down in the corner of the sofa. He reached out, clasped Shanda's hand and drew her down until she was perched woodenly on his knees. Stockinged feet flat on the floor and a flush heating her cheeks, she glared at him. In her twenty-seven years she had had some awkward moments, she told herself disgustedly, but never had she felt so foolish! And he wasn't helping matters a bit, watching her with a gleam of humor in those black eyes.

"This is ridiculous," she burst out, suddenly changing her mind. "Anyway, Lee would never buy— Oh!" She broke off as Jake spread his knees and leaned back in a lithe sprawl. She reacted instinctively, throwing her weight toward him and drawing her legs up on the cushion for support. A moment later she was lying across his thighs, her hands clutching his shoulders, her breasts pressed against his chest. He supported her with one hand across her back, the other resting proprietarily on one hip.

"We're getting more believable all the time, aren't we?" His warm chuckle was maddening.

"Pull my skirt down," she demanded, squirming as his hand passed over the bunched-up material, caressed her thigh and investigated the tender area behind her knee.

"We have just a few minutes to make this look convincing," he warned, tightening his arm.

"I can't help it. I feel so stupid! And, besides that, I'm ticklish." Her smile faded as he lowered his head, his lips softly brushing her eyebrows. Her hand rose to touch his cheek, her sensitive fingertips grazing it, savoring the rasp beneath the smooth skin. He must have to shave two or three times a day, she thought hazily.

Jake's eyes were gleaming with promise. The muscles in his broad shoulders flexed beneath her hands as he lifted her higher, closer. It was, she realized belatedly, inevitable. From their first clash that morning, it had been so. The sizzling tension, his aura of ownership, could only culminate in this moment.

His lips touched hers and she tasted the wine they had shared. That was her last rational thought. With idle curiosity, she had wondered how it would feel to kiss those firm lips. Now she knew; her body leaned into his and her lips parted in invitation as his arms accepted her slight weight. The slow movement of his tongue was a challenge that she impetuously met.

She was vaguely aware of his hands brushing over her dress. He raised his head until his mouth was just a breath away, muttering, ''Where the hell is the zipper on this thing?'' Shanda opened her eyes and stared at him. She heard the words, but the import didn't register. With an impatient twist of her body, she touched her lips to his and settled back into his arms as he uttered a pleased grunt. Just as she was beginning to wonder what on earth she was doing, she heard a loud voice.

''Shanda! What the hell's going on here?''

I wish I knew, she thought as she eased back and looked at Jake. He was gazing fixedly over her shoulder and, judging by the expression on his face, he didn't like what he saw. Obviously, Lee had made his appearance.

For a moment, she had actually forgotten about him. She squirmed in Jake's arms, managing only to twist her dress even higher, until he scooped a hand beneath her bottom and neatly turned her to face the door. He retained his hold, draping a possessive arm around her shoulders.

Shanda stiffened under Lee's affronted glare, forgetting the part assigned to her in this melodrama. Instinctively trying to move away from Jake, she was stopped by his unyielding grip on her arm. She looked up at Lee and bit back a smile.

He might as well have worn a sign on his chest. His tight pants, black tonight, she noted, clung lovingly to the muscles of his long legs and slim hips. The white shirt, with its slashed neck and full sleeves, was immediately familiar to devotees of pirate movies and had become his trademark. A chunky gold chain and medallion, which nestled in a curly thatch of golden chest hair, completed the ensemble.

Everybody knew Lee Masters, star of last year's hit TV series, "Nemesis." He was a Robin Hood of the high seas whose territory extended to whatever seaport the loosely constructed plots demanded. The show was a campy swashbuckler that captivated those hungering for wit, adventure and romance. And Lee, with his long, sun-streaked hair, daring smile and lithe, muscular body was brilliantly cast as the rope-swinging, balcony-hopping, sword-fighting hero.

Shanda continued her survey, remembering how she had become a part of his Monday-evening following, spellbound by his adroit handling of the material as he walked the fine line between tongue-in-cheek and all-out farce. She was so fascinated that she used her studio connections to wangle an introduction. The meeting had resulted in something completely unexpected and totally uncharacteristic of her. After two dates, she was engaged.

After two more, she came to her senses. Part of the problem, she rationalized, was his dimple. Even though there was just one, it was devastating. She had lost large chunks of conversation because of the tantalizing elusiveness of Mother Nature's well-placed thumbprint.

Everyone, she informed herself charitably, staring up at Lee, was entitled to one mistake. But even though hers had been of vast proportions, she had corrected it before it was too late. Or at least she tried to, she amended mentally, noting the stubborn look on his face.

For the truth was that once you got past Lee's dimple nothing much was going on. It wasn't that he was stupid, she assured herself. Just a bit superficial. He wasn't the elegant, urbane man that he portrayed, he merely believed he was. He wasn't even much of an actor. He played his role as he was told to, having neither the intelligence nor the sense of humor to understand the whimsical nature of the material. Her brief infatuation, she reminded herself for the hundredth time, should have been with the writers, or better yet, the film editors.

Maybe she could chalk the whole thing up to a delayed case of adolescence or, more properly, to the fact that she had been working on her films without stop for two years and she was lonely for male companionship. The long, grueling hours had all but eliminated her social life. She had, she remembered with a grimace, fallen for an illusion and, while she was struggling to regain her normal equanimity, Lee had decided that she was an eminently suitable fiancée for one of his stature. His decision, she recollected hazily, was based heavily on the fact that her chestnut hair contrasted beautifully with his golden mane, making them, in his opinion, a most attractive and eye-catching couple.

But an engagement, as least according to Lee's standards, had nothing to do with love and fidelity. It was a simple ploy to milk the last ounce of publicity out of a convenient situation. By their fourth date, the dimple was losing its luster, Shanda's common sense had dealt severely with her romantic inclinations, and the engagement was ended before it was even announced.

Now all she had to do, she reminded herself once again, was convince the single-minded man that they were not suited. Simple, she thought, right? Wrong. It wasn't an easy task to deliver such a message to a man recognized and admired by everyone in the country.

Everyone, apparently, except the man sitting next to her. "Who the hell are you?" he demanded.

"Lee Masters," the actor replied, waiting for applause.

Jake had the look of a man who had discovered a cockroach dogpaddling in his soup. *"He's* the one?" he asked in disbelief.

Lee accepted the astonished question as his due. "Shanda deserves the very best," he said simply, dropping gracefully to the sofa beside her. Frowning as Jake's fingers tightened proprietarily around her waist, Lee laid a tan hand on her thigh.

Feeling a bit like a wishbone, Shanda moved her leg. As she smoothed her dress, Jake shot to his feet, drawing her up to stand beside him. All of his earlier humor, she noted, had vanished. In fact, his expression would do a good job of curdling milk.

The next few minutes were going to be interesting. She'd put her money on Jake to win, but it wasn't going to be as simple as he anticipated. Coping with Lee's bullheaded belief in his own image was quite an experience for the uninitiated.

Lee's warm voice interrupted her train of thought. "Shanda, darling, come sit down and talk to me." He patted the cushion next to him. This time, as Shanda remained standing, he stared at Jake's arm, which had tightened around her waist. His gray eyes traveled slowly upward in a gaze Shanda recognized as the one the Nemesis used to intimidate his enemy. Jake was not visibly moved.

"Who are you?" Lee asked. "And what was Shanda doing in your arms when I came in?"

The voice above her head was curt. "Jake McCade. And she was in my arms because she was kissing me."

"Why?"

"Why *what?*"

Shanda sternly controlled the giggle that was threatening to escape. Jake's baffled question was nearly her undoing. It was apparent that Lee's name had meant nothing to Jake. And Jake was beginning to regard the other man with the caution that is normally reserved for an escaped lunatic.

"Why was she kissing you when she could have been kissing me?"

Good question, Shanda thought fairly. She turned back to Jake. Normally, she spoke for herself, but he had put her in this situation, assured her that she wouldn't have to say a word if she didn't want to, hadn't he? So far, she was content to let him handle it. She could always assert herself if things got bogged down too badly.

"Obviously a lack of taste on her part," Jake replied with heavy sarcasm.

"Ah. Yes. Quite."

She felt Jake stiffen at the blatant insult, then suddenly relax. She looked up to discover a gleam of amusement lurking in the dark eyes. How had she ever thought the man was humorless? she wondered, waiting for the next round.

"Probably slumming," Jake amplified outrageously.

"I see," Lee drawled, narrowing his eyes. The Nemesis, Shanda thought, unraveling an intricate plot.

"Said you made her nervous," Jake continued, piling it on with a heavy hand. "She's afraid she can't live up to your image."

"That's understandable," Lee murmured. "But she should have told me," he complained mildly to Jake, as if Shanda had ceased to exist. "I could have helped her." He leaned back, directing his attention once again to her. "Maybe a new hairstyle," he muttered. "No, I don't want it cut. Long hair photographs so well." He brightened. "Maybe you'd feel better if you lost a few pounds. I know of a terrific spa."

Shanda made a muffled sound and pressed her face against Jake's chest, her shoulders quivering. She felt a similar tremor invade his body.

"She's overcome," Jake assured the other man blandly.

"You'll get used to it, Shanda." Lee directed his hearty encouragement to her back.

"No," Jake disagreed with unabashed enjoyment, "she can't live like that. But she doesn't want you to change. Or to be any less than you already are." He pressed a ruthless hand to the back of Shanda's head as she wailed pathetically into his shoulder.

Obviously, Lee's role had not prepared him for such high tragedy. "Are you all right, Shanda?" He appealed to Jake. "Do you think she's okay? What should I do?"

"I think you ought to go back to—L.A., isn't it?—and

find someone else. Shanda's obviously not cut out for your life-style.''

Lee got up and paced the length of the sofa. Shanda had the feeling that he was eyeing her quaking form rather nervously. He decided abruptly. ''I'll come back in the morning and talk to her. Maybe she'll feel better then.''

''She won't be here in the morning.'' Jake's voice was decisive. Shanda stiffened and his arms tightened around her. ''She needs a rest and she's coming to my house to get it.''

''I'll be here in the morning,'' Lee repeated stubbornly. ''If she's not here, I'll come to your place.'' He opened the door and turned, saying, ''Oh, what'd you say your name is?''

''It's not important,'' Jake answered. ''I'm just a friend.''

The door slammed on the word ''Tomorrow.''

Jake loosened his grip, watching as Shanda wiped at her teary eyes with the backs of her hands.

''That was the most shameless thing I've ever witnessed!''

''You're right,'' he agreed, obviously not a whit repentant. ''Honey''—a reluctant grin curved his lips—''who the hell is that nitwit?''

''You really don't know,'' she marveled. ''The way you talked to him, it didn't sound as though you did.''

''He obviously thought he was someone special. I just went along with him.''

''I wronged you earlier this evening. You *don't* read the movie scandal sheets. That was none other than Lee Masters.''

''So he said. I still don't know who he is.''

''The Nemesis?'' she prompted. At his blank look, she

struck an affected fencing position. "You know, television's hero on the seven seas. Composite of Don Juan, Zorro and Robin Hood?" She saw the dawning recognition on his face.

"You mean the one that prances around in *panty hose?*"

"You got it," was the succinct reply. "Although I'm not sure he'd like the description."

"How did you meet him?"

"It's a long and rather boring story," she muttered evasively.

"All right, then try this one. How did you get engaged to him?"

"It might have been his dimple," she offered, not about to reveal either her vulnerability or her stupidity.

"Dimple?"

"Um hmm."

"What does that have to do with anything?" he asked incredulously, before he added, "I didn't see one."

She gurgled huskily, laughter welling up at his scowl. "He wasn't smiling at you," she explained reasonably. "He smiled at me a lot. And when he did, *voilà*, a gorgeous dimple."

"So gorgeous that it blinded you to the fact that there wasn't a thing behind it?"

"Temporary insanity," she pleaded, laughter still shining in her blue eyes. "Very temporary. It lasted four dates, to be exact."

"A dimple," he muttered, glaring at her in baffled disgust. He dropped down in the chair she had occupied earlier. "You'd better get packed. You heard Goldilocks. He's coming back in the morning."

"I'm not going anywhere. At least not with you. I'll get

a room in another hotel. He won't bother looking for me if it gets too inconvenient.''

"You had a reservation for this room?" It was more of a statement than a question.

"Yes."

"Well, you won't find another one. In case you hadn't noticed, there are three or four large conventions going on in the city and rooms are at a premium.''

"Then how did Lee get in?"

"Hotels usually keep a room or two open for emergencies. The unexpected arrival of celebrities falls in that category. You won't be so lucky."

"Well, I'll worry about that later. Right now, I'm going to bed."

"He said he'd be back in the morning."

"When Lee isn't working, his morning begins at the crack of noon. I'm one of those awful people who are up with the sun, so I'll have plenty of time to decide what I'm going to do."

He wasn't going to let it rest there. She could see that by the way he settled his broad shoulders against the back of the chair. But she was surprised when he didn't use his familiar steamroller tactics.

"I wish our beginning had been a little less hostile," he said slowly.

"Why, so you could have maneuvered me into bed without a struggle?"

"No." His grin was a white slash against dark skin. "I'll get you there, and the battle will just make the end result that much sweeter. It's J.B. I'm concerned about. He was looking forward to your visit and I spoiled it. He still wants you to come and stay a few days before he leaves."

"Leaves? When? For how long?"

"In a week or so. For a couple of weeks. A business trip."

She stared at him suspiciously. "Are you making this up?"

"Would I do that?" He looked at her in wounded innocence.

"Yes! I'm coming to the conclusion that you'd say or do just about anything to get what you want."

"Poor old J.B." He sighed. "There's no compassion in your heart for a lonely old man."

"Oh, come on." The words were widely spaced in exasperation. "Don't give me that pathetic-little-old-gray-haired-man routine. He looked as though he could still hold his own with you."

"Would you deprive him of relatives he didn't even know he had just because you're mad at me?"

"You fight dirty, don't you?"

"When I have to," he agreed calmly. "Family means a lot to J.B." He rose, captured her hand and walked to the door with her. "Don't deprive yourself and J.B. of something precious because you're afraid of me."

"*What?* Now just a minute, Jake McCade. You don't scare me. Not a bit."

"Glad to hear it, honey. Then there's no reason for you to refuse J.B.'s invitation, is there?" He smiled down at her. "Will you promise me something?"

"What?" The word sounded sulky, even to her own ears.

"Think about it?"

She dropped her eyes to his tie. She would go, but she'd be damned if she'd give him the satisfaction of an immediate capitulation. "All right."

"Good. Here's something else I want you to think about." He wrapped his arm around her waist, drawing her against his hard body as he slid a large hand beneath her heavy mane of hair and rested it at her nape.

"I do my best thinking when I just have one thing to concentrate on," she said nervously.

"I have faith in you," he soothed as he turned slightly and leaned back against the door, taking her with him. "You'll do just fine."

Oh, help, Shanda thought as his lips lowered to brush hers. She was drawn into the cradle of his parted legs, her body off balance and lying along his. Resting on the undeniable evidence of his arousal, she could only admire his control as his lips lightly teased, touching her lids and cheeks, then traveled back to her waiting lips.

Obviously, his experience had not been limited to tending the family oil wells. And she was reaping the benefits of his additional pursuits, she realized hazily. He had honed his technique to a fine edge during the time that she, immersed in her academic life, had decided that sex was vastly overrated and not worth altering her virginal status. The last couple of years had left her no time for involvements, even if she had wanted them. But much more of this, she realized, as his fingers laced through her hair, positioning her face for his waiting lips, and she would not only be reversing her opinion on the subject, she'd be doing it in his bed.

While she still had the strength to protest, she pressed her hands against his shoulders and pushed, trying to regain her balance. The fact that Jake now had one hand around her waist and the other cupping her firm bottom put her at a definite disadvantage, she decided. She never had been good at pushups.

"Jake, let me go," she panted. "If you want me to think about anything at all, you're defeating your own purpose." She looked up at him, her cheeks flushed, annoyed to see a teasing glint back in his eyes.

"I didn't mean you had to do it right now. Later would be just fine," he drawled, retaining his hold. "One more question."

She heaved a sigh, propped her elbows on his chest and cupped her chin in her hands. "What?"

"Where *is* the opening on this dress?"

"I'm sewn into it," she said, deadpan, daring him to push it any further.

He set her carefully on her feet. "It's a good thing I'm a patient man."

"Ha!"

He arched a dark brow. "Something you want to say?"

"No." She backed hurriedly away from the challenge. "Jake . . . what about J.B.?"

His words were short for such a patient man. "Damn it, Shanda, just be at the house tomorrow. I don't care what you do with him as long as you don't put him in front of a TV camera. And since there's no chance of that, we have nothing to worry about, do we?"

He leaned down, covered her lips in a kiss that she felt right down to her curling toes and slammed the door behind him.

Nothing to worry about. The words rumbled around the room like thunder in a sudden storm as she dimmed the lights, pulled down the underarm zipper and carefully worked her way out of the lilac dress. After wrapping a towel around her hair to keep it dry, she stepped into the shower and let tepid water run down her body.

A few minutes later, she removed the towel, dropped a

lightweight robe across the foot of the bed and climbed between the sheets nude. She was an active sleeper and had long since given up lingerie that either wrapped around her limbs or bunched around her waist.

Nothing to worry about. Good grief! She understood Jake's determination to shield J.B. from the glare of publicity, for she too valued privacy and freedom. She had a feeling, however, that Jake would not be equally understanding when he learned that she was one of those people behind TV cameras. And he would, she had no doubt of that. The way her luck was going, she thought grimly, it wouldn't take him long either.

The fact that her work was different, award-winning, would not deflect his ire, she suspected, because occasionally she did precisely the thing he seemed to abominate most—interviews.

Turning on her side and pulling the sheet over her shoulders, she thought about Jake's words. Twisting restlessly, she visualized his warm gaze becoming an icy obsidian glitter. Nothing to worry about? In a pig's eye!

Chapter Four

The sun was blazing high in the sky the next afternoon when Shanda pulled through open wrought-iron gates into a circular drive and came to a halt before a regal old house of buff-colored brick. She was reaching for her overnight case as Jake slammed the front door and loped down the sidewalk. In his faded jeans, sneakers and a knit shirt that was stretched to its limit over his shoulders, he didn't look like Oklahoma's answer to the Vanderbilts.

"You're going to have a face like a prune if you keep scowling like that," she observed as he drew up in front of her. His mood did not lighten appreciably. He stared sourly at her small case and grunted.

"Where's the rest of your luggage?"

"In the trunk, but I probably won't need it."

"I think you will. Where're your keys?"

This is getting to be a habit, she thought as, once again,

she attempted to ignore the strong, demanding hand. Penned between the hard surface of the car and his equally unyielding body, she tried once more.

"I really don't think—"

"You will," he assured her. "And it's more convenient to get them now before we put the car in the garage."

She dropped the keys in his palm and watched as he extracted two cases, balancing them easily as he closed the trunk. It's not fair, she thought darkly. The bellboy had grunted, muttering under his breath as he stuffed them in, and *he* pulls them out like toothpicks. Her brow furrowed as she mulled over Ma Nature's injustice to the feminine cause when she heaped on certain undeserving males the advantages of height, weight, strength and the innate belief in their own superiority.

Jake pocketed her keys and leaned over to place a soft kiss on her forehead. "One wrinkled person around here is enough," he chided. "Did you have any trouble with Captain Blood this morning?" he asked as he ushered her up the walk to the door.

"Lee? No. I was gone long before he was up."

"I know. I tried to call you." He slammed the door behind them. "Where have you been all day?"

"Playing tourist. I went to the National Cowboy Hall of Fame and spent hours there. It's a fascinating place."

He led her up the crimson-carpeted stairs, muttering something that sounded remarkably like "Humph!"

"You didn't think I'd taken off for parts unknown, did you?"

"It crossed my mind."

"I thought about it," she said, eyeing his broad back grimly. "When I called the desk clerk and found that you had already checked me out and paid my bill." They came to a halt beside a closed door. "I don't like that sort of high-handed nonsense, Jake. Remember, I'm your father's guest because I choose to be. You could change my mind very quickly."

His measuring gaze was enigmatic. Shanda found herself holding her breath. After a long silence, he swung open the door and nodded for her to enter. The cross words died on her lips as she stared around the large room.

"Jake, how lovely!"

The pale blue carpet complemented the watercolor pastels of the upholstery and contrasted beautifully with the paneled walls. It was definitely a woman's room. A soft, fabric-covered sleigh bed with a matching dressing table and chaise were enhanced by a dark chest and baskets of huge ferns.

"It's absolutely beautiful," she enthused, running her hand over a luxurious fur throw draped across the chaise as Jake dumped her cases on the bed. Straightening, she stood quietly, her eyes flicking around the room as she became aware of a rhythmic tapping.

Jake seemed unconcerned, so she assumed that it must be a familiar occurence, but what on earth could it be? While Jake discussed closets and bathrooms, she stepped quietly to the windows and pulled back the sheer curtains, expecting to see some activity in the garden below. Instead, she saw a huge feline, its nose pressed against the glass and its amber eyes glaring, standing on the sill demanding entry. Shanda dropped the fragile material as if the flowered pattern had suddenly sprouted thorns. Her strangled cry alerted Jake and he was braced as she flung herself at him.

"Easy, honey," he soothed as if calming a fidgety colt. "It's all right. There's nothing here that'll hurt you."

She didn't reply, merely burrowing her face in his chest and wrapping her arms around his waist, shuddering as the sinister tapping resumed.

Amusement warmed his voice. "I'm not complaining, you understand, but I sure would like to know what spooked you."

"Over there," she mumbled against his shirt, pointing to the curtains where the rapping was becoming an irritated crescendo.

"That?"

"Yes, that!" she said tartly. "There's a damned panther out there pounding on the window and you act as if it happens every day." I will murder him if he laughs at me, she decided calmly, feeling a suspicious vibration in his chest.

Jake cleared his throat. "That's just Peg," he said with commendable control. He released her and turned hastily to the window, muttering something about unlocking it.

"You're not going to let that—" Her mouth remained open as about twenty pounds of cat surged through the window and landed on the bed, skittering slightly as it slid on the luggage. Now that its face wasn't smeared all over the window, it looked considerably less alarming, she decided. It leaped off the bed, sniffed her ankle thoughtfully and sauntered out the door. Its black plumed tail rose in a disdainful hook, blatantly proclaiming its gender.

"Peg?" she inquired with an arched brow.

"For Pegasus. When we first got him, he was always at the top of a tree or on the roof. We swore he had wings."

"I've never seen a cat that big."

"He's a Maine coon cat and damned near human. The breed runs large."

"An understatement if I ever heard one. He looks as though he keeps things stirred up around here."

"He's a pain in the neck. He can climb and leap anywhere, but there's something wrong with his landing gear. We're always having to open doors and windows for him." He changed the subject abruptly. "Speaking of pains, should I expect to find the caped crusader swinging through a window in the near future?"

"Lee? I doubt it."

"I wouldn't give up so easily if you belonged to me."

"You sound very possessive."

"I am," he said flatly. "What's mine stays mine."

"Isn't it a good thing we're talking about Lee." Her voice was light, refusing the challenge. "Anyway, I don't *belong* to anyone. I'm my own person."

"You were engaged to him." His frown emphasized the disapproval in his voice.

"For my sins," she agreed. "A moment of madness, as I told you. It was the first time in a long while that I let someone make a personal decision for me. It won't happen again."

"You just chose the wrong person. He's too much of a lightweight for you. Next time—"

"I told you, there won't be a next time. I'm on the wagon, so to speak, gasping at my narrow escape. No." She returned to the original question. "Lee won't be coming around. He's a bit stubborn, but it won't be long before he believes that splitting up was his idea."

"He seems pretty determined. He could have stayed in L.A. instead of looking for you."

"He was on his way to New York. It was no big deal to stop over for a day or so. What it boils down to is that he

can't believe I'd pass up the opportunity to sit next to him
smiling into a camera for the next few months. I'm sure he
didn't expect it to last longer than that. He just didn't think
it would end before he got a flurry of publicity out of the
announcement.''

"He's an idiot." There was a wealth of disgust in
Jake's voice.

"No," Shanda disagreed, feeling contrary. "Not really. He's a nice man."

"Do me a favor?"

She arched a russet brow in inquiry.

"Don't ever refer to me as a nice man."

"I wouldn't dream of it."

He eyed her bland expression with suspicion before
asking abruptly, "Do you swim?"

"I manage. Even when I'm in over my head."

"From what I've seen, that's probably most of the
time."

"Ah, but you haven't seen that much of me."

"An oversight I'm planning to take care of." His look
was as physical as a touch.

"I walked right into that one," she admitted wryly.
"Seriously, shouldn't I go make my peace with J.B.?"

"Seriously, you should get your lovely tail into a
bathing suit. J.B. won't be here until dinner." He stopped
in the doorway. "Unless you prefer to swim without—"

"Never mind! Where should I meet you?"

"Downstairs. I'll be waiting for you."

She was opening her cases before the door closed
behind him. Rationalizing that he expected to wait, she
hung up her clothes in the closet before donning her sleek
jade maillot.

"Might as well get it over with," she muttered, rubbing her nape to ease her jangled nerves. She had been stalling, she admitted to herself, putting off the moment when those dark, unblinking eyes would survey her body.

"You're a coward," she accused herself, shrugging into a thigh-length eyelet wrap and opening the door. But she knew that whatever name she applied to herself, the man waiting at the foot of the stairs posed a threat. No doubt about it, the man was a menace. And she was too vulnerable.

She walked slowly down the stairs.

She had dreaded the first few moments by the pool, but, in retrospect, they were child's play compared to the last few minutes at the dinner table.

Jake had surprised her. After one savagely hungry look that shook her down to her toes, his straight, dark lashes lowered and he became the perfect host. They swam, soaked up the early June sun and lazily drifted from one topic of conversation to another. They agreed that a current best-selling exposé was nothing more than mud-slinging tripe, disagreed over the merits of a presidential hopeful and bickered amiably as they compared their favorite vocalists, Willie Nelson and Roger Whittaker.

It was almost, she thought later as she pulled out a long, burgundy velvet skirt and a white silk blouse, as if he were paying heed to her earlier warning. Besides, he now had her where he wanted her, on his home turf, and he could afford to move slowly. After all, does an experienced hunter panic his quarry when said quarry is moving smack dab into his trap?

"Now why," she asked her mirrored image crossly,

"did you choose such an outlandish metaphor? He isn't stalking me . . . is he?" Wishing her reflection offered more comfort than a look of stark uncertainty, she sprayed herself lightly with Chanel, buttoned the cuffs of her blouse and drifted downstairs.

Dinner passed with the ease you would expect when two urbane men on their best behavior set out to charm their guest. J.B. proved to be a raconteur par excellence; she and Jake, an appreciative audience. He spun stories of his early years in the oil fields and boom towns: of investing his meager wages, borrowing money to buy out his disgruntled partner and finally striking oil. She had the feeling that some of the excitement was lost with the advent of regular meals and a permanent roof over his head. It was like watching a Technicolor movie as J.B. verbally sketched the territory and people with an enthusiasm that was contagious.

He would be terrific in a film! Shanda allowed herself one small, wistful dream as she listened. Guiltily, she darted a look at Jake, only to find his eyes thoroughly surveying her. A slight tuck at the corner of his firm lips was the only indication that he had been caught. His warm gaze remained on her face, informing her that he approved, and left her with the distinct feeling that she had just somehow been claimed.

She looked back with a cool expression of inquiry, refusing to participate in his little game. His sharp crack of laughter coincided with the end of J.B.'s anecdote, but neither of them looked at the older man.

"I'm sorry?" She realized that J.B. had said something to her and both men were waiting, clearly expecting an answer. She turned to J.B. "I didn't hear what you said."

Just then Gladys came through the kitchen door with dessert on a tray. Shanda looked up and smiled at the angular woman she had met earlier that day. She was a distant relative of J.B.'s, a widow who now lived with the two men and ran the house.

"I made some apple pie," she said, plunking a plate down before each of them.

Shanda sniffed appreciatively but eyed the slab of pie with doubt. "Gladys, I don't think—"

"Sure you can." The words were accompanied by a friendly pat on the shoulder. "You can use a bit of fattening up."

Shanda watched the older woman disappear through the door, then turned back to find both men looking at her.

"I said," J.B. repeated patiently as if there had been no interruption, "what do you do back home?"

"Do?"

"Do. As in work," Jake said helpfully.

"Oh. Do. Well," she said, tossing it off lightly, "you know how it is in Southern California. Everyone seems to be involved either in aerospace or entertainment."

She examined the two faces before her. They each wore the same politely inquiring expression. "I work for a television studio," she stated baldly.

"Doing what?" Jake's voice was quiet, but there was something in it that tightened her nerves.

She smiled at J.B. "I'm . . . uh . . . involved in film-making." She wondered at the sudden flare of excitement in his eyes before he disciplined his expression.

Jake asked in a wintry voice, "How involved?"

"Very." She stopped herself before she launched into an explanation. If he chose to jump to the wrong conclusion, that was his problem. She would not apologize for her work. Then, turning to face him, she almost changed her mind. His anger, although contained, was palpable.

"Do you also enjoy watching TV, Shanda?" J.B.'s question broke the tension between her and Jake. "Or is that too much like a busman's holiday?"

"No, I like certain programs," she answered carefully, tilting her head to look at him. "Why do you ask?"

"I want to show you my latest toy." J.B. rose, tossing his napkin onto the table. "I'll go set it up," he said to Jake. "Bring her along when you're finished."

"I'm ready now," Shanda called to his retreating form, feeling as if she had just been tossed to a lean, hungry wolf. She rose precipitously, ready to dash headlong after the older man, only to catch her gold cuff button in the delicate lace fabric of the tablecloth.

"Damn!" she muttered as she tried to free the button with fingers that obstinately refused to obey her commands. Jake moved around the table and stopped behind her.

"Hold still," he ordered, his fingers brushing hers as he untangled the fragile threads. "I didn't say you had to stop breathing," he added grimly after a long, tense moment. Shanda held herself stiffly, trying to deny his effect on her. "There!" He removed the last tangled thread, wrapped his fingers around her wrist and turned her to face him.

"I think you owe me an explanation." His dark eyes judged, then condemned.

She shook her head in disagreement. "I promised you in the hotel that I wouldn't use my position as his guest to take advantage of your father and I won't. My profession wasn't discussed and rightly so, because it has nothing to do with the situation." She pulled her wrist away, noting absently that he had not hurt her in his determination to detain her.

Eyeing his hard expression, she burst out, "What on earth do you think I do, crank out porno flicks?"

"I was thinking more along the line of sleazy investigative reporting programs."

Shanda stiffened in anger. Sleazy! She had worked hard to get where she was and the awards she had earned were not given lightly. "Mr. Oil Tycoon," she said softly, anger deepening the blue of her eyes, "I think we'd better put some space between us before we reach the point of all-out warfare. I'm going in to see J.B. Surely you must have a bag of money stashed away that needs to be counted. Or some current magazines you should examine to be sure that no one has had the audacity to print the McCade name."

Jake watched her turn and walk out the door. He jammed his hands in his back pockets and scowled. Her rigid back was the only outward sign of her temper. He wanted to put his hands on her shoulders, to haul her back and . . . He gave a disgusted snort and strode out the other door. He wanted to get his hands on her, period.

Shanda turned to her right, more relieved than she would admit. His dark gaze had seemed to burn right through the silk of her blouse and she felt a bit like a field mouse that had just escaped the swoop of a hawk.

She heard a noise on her left, peeked in to see if J.B. was there and was once again distracted by the beauty of a room. It was spacious—huge, she amended silently. The gleam of waxed hardwood floors and the patina of old, well-preserved tables and chests blended beautifully with the bright area rugs and comfortably modern furniture. A game table was placed snugly in one corner near a billiard table. The walls not covered by books boasted a sophisticated stereo set, a TV console and an enormous fireplace.

J.B. had his back to her as he bent over a piece of equipment, muttering beneath his breath.

"What are you doing?" she asked, dropping down onto the corner of a fawn plush sofa facing the TV.

"Jake got me a VCR for my birthday several months ago and I'm still catching up on some programs I missed while I was on a trip."

Shanda leaned back, prepared to relax and enjoy herself. J.B., apparently a man of discrimination, didn't seem the type to watch game shows or tire-screeching car chases, both of which, in her opinion, made even grocery shopping seem exciting. And considering that she rarely had time to watch TV except for those Monday evenings she had hoarded while enchanted with "Nemesis," anything he played was bound to be entertaining.

Ten seconds later she was listening to the theme music of her latest film. J.B. grunted in satisfaction, turned just as her name flashed across the screen and dropped eagerly into a sturdy leather chair.

"Public TV has been doing a helluva series on the westward movement," he explained. "The first one was on the Mohawk Trail, then there was one on West Virginia and Tennessee. This is about the people who followed the Wilderness Road through the Cumberland Gap and settled in Kentucky."

Grinning at his enthusiasm, Shanda settled back and prepared to enjoy herself.

"You don't mind watching this, do you?" he asked, aware of her changing expression.

"On the contrary. I wouldn't miss it for the world."

"Our family made this trip," he mused. "That's why I wanted to—"

"Our family?" she asked.

"My daddy and *his* daddy were both born in Kentucky. The Wilderness Road was the only trail when the first McCades settled in."

The next hour passed in absorbed silence. Once again the struggles of the pioneers came to life for Shanda, but this time with a difference. *Her* family, the McCades, had been there.

"Damn good job," J.B. said at the film's end. "I wish I knew who did it. I'd like to—"

"Ahem." Shanda cleared her throat, grinning as she pointed a slim finger at the television screen.

J.B. turned just as her name filled the screen. His head swiveled back and once again Shanda caught a glint of excitement in his eyes.

"You?"

She nodded in mock modesty. "Me."

"Well, I'll be damned."

"I sincerely hope not."

He silenced the television with a flick of the remote-control switch. "Let me get this straight. You're a movie director?"

"Nope. I make documentaries."

He made an impatient gesture with his hand. "Isn't it the same thing?"

"No, there's a big difference." J.B. watched as she sat quietly, collecting her thoughts. Finally, she looked up.

"A movie director works with situations created by a writer and characters created by the writer and the actors. I work with facts. Things that really happen—or, in this case, happened, and with characters who actually lived.

My cameras are observers, catching small moments of truth and sharing them with the audience. And I have to capture the reality and reveal it creatively—or at least try to.''

One slim hand moved in a questioning gesture. "I've never tried to explain the difference before. Does that make any sense?''

He nodded. "What does Jake think about all this?'' he asked casually.

She stiffened, her eyes suddenly bright with exasperation. "Your son doesn't think. He makes assumptions. Wrong ones at that. He's the most maddening man I've ever run across.''

"Does that mean he doesn't know?''

J.B. didn't smile, but Shanda sensed his amusement. "It does. And it'll shower snowballs in hell before I explain anything to him! He's apparently decided that I do unsavory exposés. He thinks, if that's what you call his mental process, that I'm here to get you in front of a TV camera. God only knows what's supposed to happen after that.''

"He's a mite protective.'' J.B.'s tone was philosophical. Only the deep creases around his blue eyes revealed his humor. "Give him a little time. He grows on you.''

Shanda snorted.

"Where is he now?''

"I don't know,'' she said carelessly. "I told him to go away.''

J.B. chuckled. This one was going to give Jake a run for his money and he was going to be an interested spectator every step of the way.

"Tell me about your aunt,'' he said. "What does she want and how do you think I can help?''

For the second time in as many days, Shanda plunged into an explanation of Paige's quest. J.B. listened thoughtfully, nodding his head every now and then in encouragement. It was amazing, she thought, the difference a sympathetic audience made.

"But there is one thing," she concluded honestly. "Aunt Paige is hot to write a McCade history for the family and anyone else who's interested. She'd be delighted if I came up with something that would add color and spice to the story. And since she approaches the venture as an historian, she has the hide of a rhinoceros and never stops to think that others might be a bit more thin-skinned."

"Exactly what are you telling me?" Intelligent blue eyes never left her face.

"Don't tell me anything you'd prefer not to see in print," she advised bluntly. "The last thing in the world I want is to see you embarrassed or hurt."

"It would take a lot to do that."

"And what about your father?"

"What about him?"

"Has he done anything you'd rather not have made public?"

"I don't know. I have an idea we'll find out before we're through, though."

"This is going to be more awkward than I thought," Shanda complained.

"How so?"

"When I wrote to you, I had no idea you were so wealthy, so much in the public eye. It's possible that the media could pick up on my aunt's book and print excerpts out of context. You might not like that. And I know Jake wouldn't."

"Too bad," he grunted. "I don't run my life to please him." He thought for a moment. "How do you want to handle this thing?"

"I thought we'd do it as a living history. We'll put everything on tape. Whenever you have time, we'll just sit and talk. You tell me what you remember about your father, stories he might have told you about his life, anything you think would be interesting. The kinds of things you were telling us at dinner tonight would be perfect." Her enthusiasm was contagious and his eyes kindled with interest.

"That sounds painless enough. What else will you need?"

"Aunt Paige would be in seventh heaven if you have any old photos or documents."

"What kinds of documents?"

"Land grants, deeds, anything that would help place your father or his parents in a particular place at any given time."

"Hmm. I'll have to give that one some thought." He ran a hand through his thick white hair, making it stand on end.

"When do you think we could get started?" Shanda asked, trying to curb her impatience.

"Maybe in a day or so," he murmured, looking beyond her as he thought. "I have a few things to clear up first. You're on your vacation, aren't you?"

She nodded.

"Well, why don't you just relax and enjoy yourself for the next few days. Let Jake entertain you."

"I don't think that's a very good idea," she said slowly. "Jake and I don't exactly—" She stopped, finding it difficult to explain what exactly they didn't do.

"I can keep busy without his help," she continued briskly. "Aunt Paige wanted me to stop in at the historical society and go through microfilms of some old newspapers. And there are several other things," she added vaguely, thinking of Buell's mysterious marital status. She would be visiting the county clerk's office to request divorce documents.

"You're not going to let him spook you, are you?"

She met the oddly challenging look in J.B.'s eyes with one of determination. "No way," she said succinctly as she got up from the sofa, smoothing her long skirt over her hips. "I didn't get where I am by caving in at the first obstacle. Your son has the mistaken idea that all he has to do is snap his fingers and I'll jump."

She directed a brilliant smile at J.B. and said softly, "I quit jumping a long time ago."

J.B.'s amused gaze followed her straight-backed exit. Life at the house and ranch had been quiet and predictable for too long now. He had an idea things were about to change.

Chapter Five

Despite her brave words, Shanda looked around cautiously before ascending the stairs to her room. She wasn't afraid, she assured herself, she merely believed that sometimes discretion was indeed the better part of valor.

She turned the knob quietly, slipped into her room and came to a startled halt. She dubiously eyed an enormous black pelt draped over the back of a blue Queen Anne wing chair. Two amber eyes slitted open, leisurely inspected her, then closed again in lazy comfort.

"How'd you get in here, Peg?" Shanda skirted the large cat as she withdrew a blue caftan from the closet and headed for the bathroom. "Don't get too comfortable," she warned before closing the door. "You're not spending the night."

Fifteen minutes later, clad in the caftan and carrying the clothes she had worn earlier, she returned. The cat was still propped comfortably on the high-backed chair, facing the television and seeming to absorb the quietly spoken words of a local news team.

Shanda's voice came from within the closet as she carefully hung up her clothes. "I don't know how you did that," she said with a touch of admiration, "but it still doesn't get you a room for the night. I'm going to bed. You can turn off the TV and let yourself out the same way you got in."

"Well, that's clear enough." Jake's deep voice startled her. "But it lacks a certain element of welcome. Is that the way you always say good night?"

Four steps brought Shanda to the side of the chair. Jake looked up at her with a lazy smile. Her voice was serene, ignoring her body's response to his softened look. "No. Sometimes I'm even more to the point." Her tone cooled abruptly as she remembered. "What are you doing here?"

"Watching the news. I want to see the weather report."

"Go watch your own TV."

"I can't. It has to be this one."

"Why?"

"Because it's in your room and I have to talk to you."

"You've already said quite enough for one evening," Shanda said coolly.

His dark gaze lingered on the luxuriant hair falling over her shoulders, and reluctantly moved up to her taut face. His warm fingers closed over hers and he lifted her hand to his mouth, softly dropping a kiss on the inside of her wrist.

"I'm sorry about that." His grip tightened as he felt her resist. "Honey, my trusting mechanism has grown rusty over the years. Especially where J.B. is concerned. That's why I came in here. I wanted to apologize."

His rueful expression amused her. He obviously wasn't

used to suffering from foot-in-mouth disease and didn't quite know how to handle it. But if their relationship so far was any indication, he'd better learn—and fast!

"Is that the way it always is?" she asked wryly, knowing she was softening. "You apologize and peace reigns until you think of more insults?"

"I guess I deserve that. But what more do you want?" he asked, bending his head and once again bringing her wrist to his lips.

"Nothing! Apology accepted," she said quickly, tugging at her hand. Her blood was still singing from his last gentle assault and she wasn't prepared to risk another.

"Thank you." He grinned up at her. "Now that that's over, why don't you join me?"

She looked doubtfully at the lithe form filling the graceful chair. "There's no room. I'll sit over here."

"It's not like you to overlook the obvious," he said, tugging gently at her hand. "You'll fit in my lap just fine."

Shanda dug her bare feet into the thick rug, leaning back in resistance. She knew by the gleam of amusement lighting his dark eyes that he was aware that her body was bare beneath the silky caftan. And that he was enjoying her predicament. Taking advantage of her hesitation, he tugged again, toppling her into his lap.

"See? There's plenty of room."

She glared up at him. Then, with a twist of her hips, she bent her knees and turned to face the TV.

He moved his hands, resting one on her arm and one on her slim leg, just below her knee. She wiggled again, reminding him of a ruffled chick, flouncing and smoothing its feathers.

Shanda watched the screen flicker but was too aware of the muscular body so easily supporting her own to make any sense of it. How did he do it? she wondered. Why did this particular man have such a paralyzing effect on her tongue? She had always been strong-willed and independent. She handed over the running of her life to no one. Yet this man had walked through the door, directed that farcical scene in the hotel with Lee, and now had her sitting on his lap nearly naked.

Jake's nostrils flared as he caught the elusive scent of lemon. She smelled almost as delicious as she felt. He dipped his head, touching the tip of her ear with his lips as he slid his right arm around her waist. His left hand closed on her ankle. She stiffened, but apparently not in protest, he thought. He drew her closer, smiling.

"Did you see *that?*"

"Ouch!"

Their voices merged as her head jerked back, hitting his chin. She turned to face him, rubbing the back of her head.

Jake glared down at her. "Damn it! What's the matter with you?"

"Didn't you see?" Shanda was almost stuttering in agitation. "It said a tornado is coming!"

Jake watched the television screen intently and finally leaned back in a relaxed slouch. "It's not a warning. It's only a tornado watch."

Her voice rose an octave and she looked at him as if he had sprouted another head. "You mean people around here just sit and *watch* them?"

Grinning at her reaction, he said in a voice meant to soothe, "I'm just saying it's not dangerous. Yet."

"Well, I'm not hanging around until it gets that way." She pulled out of his arms and stood up. "I'm going to get dressed."

"What for?"

"If I'm going to be sucked up in a funnel," she said, disappearing into the closet, "I'm at least going to have some clothes on." The caftan came flying out of the closet and she followed it almost immediately, dressed in jeans and a sweater. Sliding her feet into shoes, she said, "And you can wipe that grin off your face. You may not be worried, but I'm heading for the storm cellar."

She stopped, alerted by his startled expression. "That is if you'll tell me where it is," she continued slowly.

"We don't have one."

Blank astonishment crossed her face as she absorbed his words. "I don't believe it," she said, stupefied. "You've got this great rattling mansion on top of a hill and you don't even have a *storm cellar?*"

"Our neighbors don't either," he offered in consolation.

"Look," she said as if speaking to a person of limited understanding, "I grew up watching reruns of *The Wizard of Oz. Everyone* in this part of the country has them. They come with the territory. And everyone *uses* them. Except that stupid dog, Toto, and he got just what he deserved." She scowled as he bit back a grin. "Why don't you have one?"

"We've never needed it," he said simply. "Shanda, this place is over fifty years old and it's never been touched. You'll be safe here."

"There's always a first time." She snatched up a pillow and the fur throw on the chaise. "You don't by any chance have a basement, do you?" she inquired politely.

"Of course we do. But, honestly, it isn't necessary."

"As long as that little strip running along the bottom edge of the television screen says that a tornado is coming, I'll be in the basement." She raised one eyebrow. "Will you show me the way or shall I go downstairs and peek through doors until I find it?"

Peg jumped down, rubbed against Shanda's ankles and headed for the door. Once there, he stared at the doorknob, then twitched his tail and turned to stare at them. Shanda could almost hear him asking, "Well, what are we waiting for?"

Peg led the way, taking the stairs in mad leaps. Jake had relieved Shanda of the pillow and cover, but that was all he had accomplished.

"No." Shanda shook her head. "You stay up here and get blown away. I'll brave the cobwebs." A moment later she was being led down another set of stairs and into a fully equipped gymnasium. "I might have known. I'd have to bring in my own spiders to find a cobweb in this house."

Jake looked down at her in exasperation. "You really do amaze me. You live in a state where the ground buckles beneath your feet and houses slide into the ocean, yet you panic at the thought of a twister."

She shrugged. "It's all a matter of what you're used to, I guess. I have more sense than to buy a house on a hill ten feet away from the water, and earthquakes sneak up on you. They're over almost before you have a chance to worry."

Jake led her into a small room with a single bed. "Will this be okay?"

"As long as it doesn't fly through the roof, it's terrific." She kicked her shoes off, sat down on the bed and reached up to get the pillow and cover. "Thank you," she said, arranging them to her satisfaction. "See you in the morning—if you're still around." She grinned as he raised his brows and shook his head.

"Hey," she called to his retreating figure, "come back and get your friend." She pointed to the distorted lump circling under the cover and finally settling in the curve of her waist. Padded paws gently kneaded her stomach and a rumbling purr rose a decibel or so.

Jake looked back. *"Your* friend," he said with cool mockery. "He broke into your room and he's sharing your bed. No friend of mine would get away with that." He turned away and took the stairs two at a time, shaking his head in disbelief. He was envious of a damn cat!

Four hours later, he stood looking down at Shanda as she slept. Her hair was dark against the pillow. The cover had slipped down to her waist and he saw that her fingers were entwined in the long fur of the blissfully sleeping cat.

Without a flicker of remorse, Jake dislodged Peg, ignoring his grumbling complaint as he landed on the floor. He slid his hands beneath Shanda and lifted her. She murmured drowsily and he held her closer. "It's okay, honey. You can go back to your own bed now."

He shouldered her bedroom door open and scowled as Peg slipped in before him. He set Shanda carefully on her feet and supported her while he drew back the blankets on the bed.

"What time is it?" she asked, blinking in the dim light.

"About two."

"What are you doing up at this hour?"

"Putting you to bed."

"I can manage, thanks." She was waking up slowly, but was still aware of the gleam in his watchful eyes. She might be sleepy, but she wasn't unconscious! "I'm a big girl now."

"So I've noticed." His gaze was enigmatic as he watched her fingers lace through her disheveled waves, trying to subdue them. "You won't fall asleep in your clothes, will you?"

"I never sleep in clothes," she answered vaguely.

With a quick intake of breath, he turned sharply and moved to the door. "Come on, Peg," he ordered. "Let's give the lady some privacy."

"He's okay," Shanda objected sleepily. "I don't mind."

Jake glared back at the cat. Peg, with great deliberation, jumped up on the bed, walked to the center and sat facing the door. He yawned, showing his fine, pointed teeth. His slitted amber eyes never left the man in the doorway.

Jake stood in the hall looking at the closed door. Outmaneuvered by a cat! For this he had stayed up watching the news until all threat of the tornado disappeared? To carry Shanda's warm and trusting body upstairs and leave her in the possession of a cat! No way! Tomorrow, he vowed, Shanda St. James was going to learn that under her cool, self-contained shell, there was a woman waiting to ignite—at his touch.

Lesson number one, Miss St. James. Tomorrow!

"What do you think?" Shanda asked, looking up as Jake approached. Her own thoughts were far from her question. The man should be banned from appearing in public like that, she decided. The dark, springy hair on his broad chest arrowed down and disappeared into his excuse of a bathing suit. His long, strongly muscled legs carried him swiftly toward her. Collecting her rattled thoughts, she smiled up at him.

"If you had to label this picture, what would you call it?" Shanda was lying on her side on a chaise longue at the edge of the pool. Peg was lying on the ground beside the chair, flat on his back, unmoving as Shanda lightly traced her finger from his throat to his stomach and back again. He seemed to be in an ecstatic trance, his mouth stretched into a grin and his legs folded limply against his body.

"Blissful idiocy," Jake grunted as he stopped beside them. "And I'd be in just about the same condition if you were stroking me that way."

Shanda snatched her hand away as if she had touched a hot wire, turned on her back and quickly changed the subject. "You look tired. Didn't you sleep well last night?"

"I worked overtime yesterday. I was carrying a body around the house at two in the morning. Scoot over," he commanded, lowering himself to the chaise, nudging his hips against hers until she shifted. Sighing in contentment, he stretched out beside her.

Peg, obviously feeling abandoned, climbed up the trunk of a nearby maple tree and crouched overhead on a thick limb, almost hidden behind the large, shimmering green leaves.

Shanda chuckled. "Sounds like something out of a horror movie. Anyway, aren't you supposed to let sleeping bodies lie?"

"Dogs," he corrected. "Besides, if I'd had anything to say about it, that particular body would have been lying in my bed beside me. But it had a strange fixation about cellars and basements."

"Hmm, sounds like you run a mighty strange setup around her, podner," she drawled. The effect she strove for was ruined when her spine connected with the metal frame of the lounge chair and she wiggled in discomfort. "With all the chairs around here, I don't know why you have to hog the biggest part of mine," she complained.

"Aren't you comfortable?" he asked in mock concern. "Here, let me help you."

Before Shanda could protest, before she even thought of it, he turned on his side and gently pulled her to face him. "There. How's that?"

She looked at him from a distance of two inches and stiffened. Blinking, she shut out the sight of his firm lips so close to her own. "It's not exactly what I had in mind." She tried to convince herself that her voice wasn't a breathless whisper and failed miserably.

"You're all tense," he admonished, massaging her neck and the shoulder that wasn't trapped beneath her. "I thought you were on vacation. You've got to learn to relax."

She closed her eyes again, clenching her jaws to hold back a stream of irritated words. How do you relax, she asked herself, when you're *glued* to a man from your eyebrows to your toenails?

"I *was* relaxed. Five minutes ago I felt as though I didn't have a bone in my body."

"In that case, you can do it again. Here, I'll help. All you have to do is rest your head on my shoulder and take a few deep breaths." Once again she was shifted. Automatically following his instructions, she noted that his deeply appreciative gaze was resting on her breasts. Almost choking on an indrawn breath, she coughed, seeking frantically for an innocuous topic of conversation. Anything would do, she reasoned. At least anything that would change his focus of concentration.

"Whose idea was it to have the pool so near the trees?" she wondered aloud. "I like it. It's much nicer than having umbrellas stuck in concrete decking."

He shrugged. "Mine. Of course, it plays hell with the pool and the filter, but that's okay. It's worth it."

"And, of course, you can afford to hire a guard to stand by with a net and vacuum to whip out any leaves that dare to fall in."

She felt him nod slowly. "Two, if necessary." Craning her neck to look up at him, she caught the trace of a smile on his lips.

"I'm relaxed," she announced abruptly. "Can I have my chair back now?"

"In a minute," he murmured, plucking off her sunglasses and placing them on a nearby table. "I came out to have a word with a certain fast-talking lady from Malibu."

"The only fast thing around here is your hand," she said definitely, removing the large, warm hand that had journeyed down her arm to her thigh and was heading for her stomach.

"What have you been up to?" Jake asked abruptly. "J.B.'s walking around like a cat licking cream off his whiskers."

"I don't know why he should be," she said in honest surprise. "All we talked about was Aunt Paige and her blasted book."

"And he's trying to get rid of me."

Mirth welled up within her at his complaint and Shanda giggled irrepressibly. "I told him you were a pain in the neck, but I didn't expect him to put a contract out on you.''

"Very funny." He examined her face, his dark eyes not missing a thing. "And very peculiar. He's had this trip set up for several months now and all of a sudden he wants me to go in his place. How do you explain that?"

"I can't," she said simply. Grateful that she had a clear conscience, Shanda looked up at him. J.B. was a wily old bird and obviously had something up his sleeve. And, just as obviously, it was something he preferred not to discuss with Jake.

"I wish I knew," he said slowly.

"What?"

"Exactly what you're up to."

Suddenly, she was tired of the whole thing. "For heaven's sake, is it so hard to believe that I'm exactly what I say I am?"

"Yes." Then as clearly as if he had said the words aloud, she knew what was coming. "But I can handle it." His hand fell to her shoulder and he shifted until he was leaning over her. "And I can handle you."

Feeling more than a little claustrophobic, she said sharply, "That sounds like something out of a bad movie. I told you how I felt about being handled."

"Um hmm," he murmured absently, looking her over in a way that made her pulse leap. Without exerting any pressure at all, he held her motionless. His lips touched lightly at her temple and his warm breath brushed her cheek, her chin. She hardly breathed as his mouth moved to the racing pulse at her throat and down to the taut swell above her top.

"Jake." The word was a whisper from between dry lips.

"Hmm?"

"I don't think—"

His lips touched the shadowy cleft between her high, firm breasts and her mind ceased functioning. His breath warmed her flesh as she struggled to collect her shattered thoughts. She had been saying something important, vital . . . Ah, she had it now. . . .

"that this is—"

She stopped again as his mouth softly traced her satiny flesh along the top of her suit, starting at one side, dipping in the center and rising to the other side.

". . . a very good idea," she ended with a gasp. But from the sweet, boneless state of her body, she knew she couldn't stop him. Not by herself. Unless some heavenly intervention occurred soon, *very* soon, she was in big trouble.

"Uhff!"

Pressed back into the chaise by the weight of Jake's body, she grunted. Something had happened all right. It felt as though a fifty-pound bag of cement had landed on Jake. She felt the shock ripple through his body as he tightened his muscles and arched over her protectively.

The next few moments were a confusing mixture of sounds. Jake was swearing lustily, the branch overhead lashed noisily, and above all that was the loud, contented purr of a cat. She opened her eyes to the sight of a black, furry face peering over Jake's shoulder, looking down at her with interest. She had heard of angels in disguise, but this was ridiculous!

Shanda's lively sense of humor had gotten her into trouble more than once. She had tried, really tried, to subdue it. But once the humor of a situation struck her, she was lost to all sense of propriety.

Covering her face with her hands to shut out the sight of Jake's astonished anger, she felt the tremors start in her stomach and radiate upward. A gurgling sound coming from behind her fingers startled Jake into silence.

The sight of tears seeping through her fingers renewed his emphatic stream of words. "Oh God, you're hurt! Lie still, let me see if anything's broken. I've never known that damn cat to fall out of a tree before," he muttered distractedly as his hands brushed methodically over her legs, rib cage and arms. Easing her up slowly, with an arm behind her shoulders, he said, "Come on, honey, you're okay."

He shifted her sideways on the chaise until her feet touched the ground and squatted before her. Frowning, he listened to her wheezing gasps. "Shanda, you're okay," he said again, reaching for her hands. "You're . . . *laughing?*"

"I'm sorry." She attempted to apologize as she brushed away her tears, then whooped anew at his stunned expression. She tried again in a few moments. "It was just so funny. If you could have seen your face!"

Nervously eyeing his now expressionless face, she rattled on. "Something just came over me and I couldn't help myself. I really am sorry."

"I understand perfectly," he said, standing up. "It happens to me at times. In fact, I feel it coming on right now." He picked her up without effort and walked toward the deep end of the pool.

Shanda's tone was sweetly reasonable as she said, "You're not really going to toss me in the water, are you, Jake? All because I laughed a little?" Her voice rose an octave as he kept on walking. "Jake? Jake! That water's cold! My hair will clog your filter! My suntan oil will make the water greasy. You'll have an awful time cleaning it!''

''Lady . . .'' His voice was quiet, a touch of amusement coloring it. ''Whatever it takes, it's going to be worth it!'' His muscles tensed and, at the last moment, Shanda threw her arms around his neck, pulling him in with her. As they hit the water, sinking to the bottom, she struggled to free herself. Instead, she was pinned against him, her legs confined by his, her body held easily in his strong arms. Opening her eyes, she saw him dip his head and then his cool lips covered hers. When they emerged—and it could have been seconds or hours later—her ears were ringing from lack of air and she was clinging weakly to his broad shoulders.

It didn't take her long to recover. ''You idiot! You could have drowned us!''

Grinning in satisfaction, Jake admitted, ''I've always wanted to try that.'' He nudged her to the side of the pool, got out and reached down to help her up. He draped an arm around her shoulders and led her back to the chairs. When she had seated herself and sternly pointed to another chair for him, he continued. ''It does have its limitations, though. We probably weren't down there for thirty seconds.''

He ignored her strangled sound of protest. ''Now if we had been in that chair''—he pointed to where she was comfortably stretched out—''who knows how long that kiss might have lasted. We might still be—''

''Don't you ever think of anything else?'' she interrupted desperately, reaching for the glass of iced tea on the table beside her.

''Sure I do. I think of taking off your clothes, piece by piece, until that gorgeous body is just as nature created it.

I think of stroking every square inch of your honey-gold flesh. I think of taking you to bed and warming you with my naked body." He leaned back with a frustrated sigh. "And that, lady, is just for starters!"

Shanda's glass slipped out of her hand to the grass below as she stared at him. Shaken by his words, she willed her hand to remain steady as she picked it up. Jake reached for it at the same time and she jerked away as their hands touched.

"What is it with you?" he asked. "You must be twenty-nine or thirty—"

"Twenty-seven!" she snapped an instant before she realized she had neatly fallen into his trap.

"Twenty-seven," he continued smoothly, "and unless you're scared to death or half asleep, you don't even want me touching you. You act like a skittish virgin."

Scarcely breathing, her startled gaze met his and she could feel the color staining her cheeks.

"Well, I'll be damned." He exhaled slowly, then drew in a sudden breath.

Shanda stood up and shrugged into her light terry jacket. Her voice was cool, defying him to say another word on the subject. "I suppose I'll see you at dinner?"

He nodded, still speechless, watching as she moved proudly toward the house. Peg trotted at her side, managing to look like a temporarily tamed panther. Jake's brows drew together in a frown. He felt as if the cat had landed on his head instead of on his back. So she really had avoided the fast lane. In her line of work, that must have taken some fancy footwork. And that damn cat had *never* fallen out of a tree!

Oblivious to the warm breeze carrying the sweet fragrance of budding flowers, he sat for a long time staring absently at his crossed bare feet. Not since he was sixteen had he felt such a surge of desire for a woman. Never had he felt so protective of one. If another man touched Shanda as he did, he would throttle him. Slowly and with great pleasure.

He picked up the sunglasses she had left behind. It had been well executed, but there was no doubt in his mind that she had definitely retreated. His grin faded as he remembered how she responded with such astonishing sensuality to his touch. For the first time in his life he had met a real woman, one who wasn't interested in his money. Also, for the first time, he cared whether he won or lost the battle.

Chapter Six

After dinner that evening, the three of them moved to the den. J.B. seemed lost in thought, not bothering to referee the sparring match between the other two.

"So when did you start your vacation?" Jake asked in an affable tone.

Shanda ignored the verbal olive branch. "When I finished my last bit of sleaze," she answered calmly, her eyes meeting his in a silent challenge.

"And when do you have to go back?"

"When I start my next one." She bit back a smile of satisfaction as he got up impatiently and walked to the window.

He turned around and sat down beside her on the sofa. "I apologized for that crack. I still don't know what you do and it's obvious that you're not going to tell me now. But whatever it is, I'm sure you do it well."

She thought of the Emmy nomination for her last

documentary and nodded. "Thank you. Apology accepted."

"But what I can't understand," he added idly, "is how, at twenty-seven, you can still be—"

She turned and examined him with eyes so cold that they should have left him with frostbite. "Be what?" Her question was soft and furious.

A dark brow rose in bland surprise. "Single," he said. "I thought the men in California moved faster than that."

"You've got a few years on me," she answered with a touch of asperity, "and I don't hear the patter of little feet around here."

J.B. broke into the hostilities. "When are you leaving for Texas, Jake?"

"I didn't know it was settled that I was going. I have a guest here in the house, you know," he reminded the older man, ignoring Shanda's start of surprise.

"I know. I'll take care of her while you're gone."

"You mean this isn't your house?" Shanda asked J.B.

"I deeded this place over to Jake a long time ago. I live at the ranch."

"What ranch?"

"The one in Buellton."

"Where's that?" Shanda asked, beginning to feel like the straight man in a vaudeville routine.

"South of here," J.B. answered. "My daddy built the ranch house and the town just sort of grew up around it." He nodded as if reaching a decision. "I think I'll take her out to the ranch while you're gone," he said to Jake.

"Damn it all, J.B., hold on just a minute. You set up this trip. It concerns your end of the business, not mine. I'm not running around the country to handle deals that I know nothing about."

"You know oil and you know men. It's only the leases for the Jurgens, Cole and Perkins land."

"Only? You've been working with them for three months and now you expect me to waltz in and just get their signatures? It won't work, J.B. Especially with Cole. You know he's as independent as a hog on ice. If you don't show up, I'll be starting from scratch and it'll be an uphill battle all the way."

Shanda watched the two men with interest. J.B. was as smooth as cream, and Jake was furious. She had the feeling that the younger man rarely found himself at a disadvantage in his business dealings and she was intrigued by his objections. It was also, she admitted to herself, a pleasure to watch him try to maneuver himself out of a losing situation. Because that's definitely what it was. With anyone else, he would issue a resounding "No!" and that would be that. In this case, his affection for J.B. was eliminating that option.

"I'll call them," J.B. said quietly.

Jake wasn't satisfied. "Why aren't you going?" he asked bluntly.

"Because I want to spend some time with Shanda. You can't expect a pretty young thing like her to hang around forever waiting for an old man. Besides, I promised to help her."

The pretty young thing thought it was time to join the fracas. Schooling her face to innocence, she turned to Jake. "You did tell me how important J.B.'s family was to him." She opened her eyes wide and smiled, stopping just short of fluttering her lashes. And received a black scowl for her effort.

Jake stood up irritably. "All right. I'll go. Give me your files and let me look through the stuff. But I'll warn you right now, I don't have time to chase the three of them around the country. I have a business of my own to run.''

"Thanks, son," J.B. said quietly. "I knew I could count on you. The files are on my dresser if you want them now.'' He watched Jake veer away and only the slight lift at the corner of his mouth betrayed him.

"You old wolf," Shanda said admiringly. "I once told Jake that he fought dirty. Now I see where he learned all his tricks.'' She shifted to a more comfortable position, folding one leg beneath her. "I have a feeling that there's more to this than meets the eye. I would have waited for you to come back. Unless you were going to be gone for several months.''

"I know that. And what's making Jake so mad is that he knows it, too. He just can't figure out what's going on.''

"Neither can I," Shanda pointed out. "And I have the feeling that I'm a lot more involved than he is.''

They eyed each other levelly. J.B. finally shrugged and said, "I want to ask a favor, but I want you to see the ranch first.''

"Why wait? You know I'll do it.''

He smiled warmly at the picture she made as she sat curled up on the couch. She looked so young. Not nearly old enough to have the skills he needed. And, he thought with amusement, the way Jake was walking around pawing the ground, that wasn't all she had.

"Thanks, honey. That's a generous offer. Especially since you don't even know what I want.''

"I trust you," she said confidently. "But I wish I knew why you're so determined to get Jake out of the way for a while.''

"Jake's a good man to have on your side when the

going gets tough. But you might have noticed that he has a tendency to want things his way?'' J.B. grinned as she nodded emphatically. ''I turned the biggest part of the business over to him some time ago, but he acts as though I turned in my horse sense at the same time. There're still a few things I like to do without him poking around. And this is one of them.''

His blue eyes gleamed with amusement. ''Besides, it's nice to know I can still make him jump.''

Shanda chuckled. ''That was a jump? It looked more like a classic case of heel-dragging to me.''

''You're right. But at least he moved.'' J.B. stood up. ''I'm going to turn in. Jake should be down in a few minutes, but in the meantime make yourself at home.''

''Come on, J.B.,'' Shanda coaxed. ''My curiosity is killing me. What's the favor you want?''

''Plenty of time for that. You just relax and take it easy for a day or so.''

''Will blackmail help?''

''I doubt it,'' he said from the doorway. ''Can't think of a thing I'd pay good money to keep anyone from finding out.''

''Heck.'' She sighed gustily as he turned away. ''Good night, Jocelyn Beverly,'' she called softly, then sat back with an expectant look. She didn't have long to wait.

Moving with the speed of a much younger man, J.B. reappeared in the doorway. ''How in the sweet hell did you find that out?''

''Aunt Paige knows all, tells all,'' Shanda chanted.

''Damn,'' he said mildly. Looking at her with a thoughtful expression, he said, ''I don't believe in encouraging blackmailers, but I'm not above a bit of bribery.''

"I suppose I should stick to my guns, but I'm new at this kind of thing. What do you have to offer?"

"How about access to an attic full of stuff at the ranch, all belonging to my daddy? Papers, diaries, things that were put up there when he died. No one's ever gone through any of it."

"Papers? Diaries?" She almost stuttered in her excitement.

"Who knows, you might come across something interesting. Well, I'm for bed," he announced, sternly controlling a grin at her dazed expression. "See you in the morning."

"Good night," she murmured absently. *Diaries!* And who knew what else. Visions of old photographs, birth certificates and a family Bible danced an elated little jig in her head. And, of course, the very first thing she would find would be a framed copy of Buell's divorce from wife number one!

Shanda felt a pang of regret. How Aunt Paige would have loved to be right in the middle of this. She glanced at her watch and nodded in satisfaction. With the two-hour time difference, it was still early enough to make a telephone call to California. The good news would perk her aunt up. As Shanda headed for the door, her mind was flitting ahead. She'd go to her room, make a collect call to her aunt and have a nice, long chat.

Moving faster now that her decision had been made, she rounded the corner and careened right into Jake. Jolted, she stood quietly, held in place by his large hand on her shoulder, watching as papers fell from the file he carried, sliding and skittering across the highly waxed floor.

Crawling on their hands and knees, they retrieved the

papers. Jake glanced up as Shanda reached for the last piece, which had insinuated itself between the wall and a sturdy chair. His fascinated gaze never left her as she maneuvered into position. First, she shoved the chair, muttering darkly when it wouldn't budge. Then, bending until her chest touched her knees and her skirt clung tightly to the rounded curves of her hips and thighs, she eased her arm behind the chair. Her fingertips touched the corner of the paper and she strained to gain an extra fraction of an inch. Mumbling in frustration, she stretched full length on the floor and tried once again.

Tilting her head to one side, she saw that Jake was sitting cross-legged, appreciatively eyeing the considerable length of shapely leg revealed by her scrunched-up skirt.

"Will you quit gawking," she gritted, "and get over here and help me."

Reluctantly giving up his front-row, center seat, Jake stood, walked over and easily moved the chair. Shanda grabbed the paper, handed it to him and rose, smoothing her skirt. She turned away, heading for the door, when Jake enclosed her hand in his.

"Where are you going in such a hurry?" Giving her no time to answer, he slid his hand up her arm and curved it around her shoulder, turning her back toward the den. He led her into the room, closed the door and urged her over to the sofa. Retaining his grip on her shoulder, he dropped down on the plush cushions, taking Shanda along with him.

"Well?" he demanded.

"Well, what?"

"What was the big rush?"

"You make it sound as though I were running around like a mad woman."

"You almost knocked me down."

"As if I could. Anyway, it was only because you weren't looking where you were going." Ignoring his look of disbelief, she continued. "I was just going to call Aunt Paige."

"Do you call her every day?"

"No. Just when I have something excit—only every now and then to keep in touch," she ended lamely. It had belatedly occurred to her that he might be a tad irate to learn that she was going to rummage through J.B.'s attic.

He examined her face closely. "I thought so."

"What?"

"Cream."

She arched her brows questioningly.

"Cream," he repeated accusingly. "On your whiskers. Just like J.B." He stared down at her in frustration. "What the *hell* are you two up to?"

"Don't be so nosy," she recommended, shifting a bit to get some breathing space. "Anyway, it's absolutely innocent, I promise. Why don't you quit playing super-sleuth and just let J.B. have some fun? You're his son, remember? Not his father."

After a long silence, during which Shanda felt as though Jake's eyes were boring right into her, he sighed and leaned back, his shoulders touching hers. "All right," he conceded, once again capturing her hand. "But since you seem to have him wrapped around this"—he separated her fingers and gently touched her smallest finger—"it would be nice if I knew something about you. So, come on, give."

"But I told you," she protested.

"You told me all about Aunt Paige. I want to know every last thing about Shanda St. James."

"All right," she said, sighing extravagantly. Once again she shifted, trying to work some space in between them. Was the dratted man doing it deliberately? she wondered. Each time she managed to gain an inch or two, he eliminated the empty space without even seeming to move. "I was born in Southern California," she began, then faltered as his arm once again touched hers. All right, she thought, suspiciously examining his expressionless face. If he wants a life story, he'll get one.

"I took my first step at nine months and—"

"You can skip the next few years."

"Are you sure? You'll miss my adventures with the tooth fairy and Santa."

"I'll risk it. Go on."

"I went to preschool and brought home marvelous paint-smeared papers—"

"Jump about ten years."

"I got braces when I was fourteen and blinded everyone in sight when I smiled. My brothers said I—"

"Tell me about your family," he suggested, resting his hand on her thigh.

"One mother, one father," she continued gamely. "Still married and still crazy about each other. One older brother, one younger. Both married. One lives in Nevada, one in Oregon."

"You can skip the cheerleading and homecoming queen bit," he said, his thumb tracing a lazy pattern on her thigh. "Start at college and keep on until you get to Oklahoma."

She cleared her throat, watching his hand as if it were a snake. She should really do something about that, she thought. Or should she? That "skittish virgin" still smarted and the last thing she wanted to do was to give him more ammunition to aim at her.

"Aunt Paige," she began slowly, "was a strong role model for me. I followed in her footsteps and majored in history." She casually crossed her legs, shifting fractionally, and noted with satisfaction that his hand slid from her thigh to the plump cushion of the sofa. Her sense of well-being had barely registered when he moved again.

"And?" Jake asked, turning to face her, resting one arm along the back of the couch behind her head, his legs shifting, conforming to hers.

And what? she wondered, feeling the warmth of his body from her shoulders to her ankles. Blood shot to her head and sang crazily in her ears, its roar drowning out any other sound. Her skin felt hot, reminding her of the last time she had had the flu. She doubted, however, that there was a simple antidote to this malady.

Was there such a thing as an anti-Jake injection? she mused hazily. Or perhaps a pill she could take daily until she was about a hundred miles away from him? Noticing his light and rapid breathing, she decided that whatever she had, it seemed to be contagious.

"Jake."

"Hmm?"

"I think I ought to save the story of my life for some other time."

"Right." His lips touched the sensitive skin at the corner of her eye.

She jumped involuntarily. "I mean it's getting late and you probably have things you want to do."

"Exactly." His breath was warm on her face as his lips slid from her cheekbone to her chin.

"To get ready for your trip."

"First things first," he murmured, bending his finger to tilt her chin, raising her face to his.

Oh, boy! she thought. No more fun and games. This time he means business. Too bad he's only looking for a bed part—Her thoughts splintered into minute particles as his lips settled gently on hers. The kiss was a soft, exploratory inquiry, demanding an answer.

"What's the question? was her first thought, followed immediately by *who cares?* Her hands touched his shoulders and then her arms wrapped around his neck in the time it took her to switch from no to maybe to yes.

Shanda was vaguely aware of Jake's arm slipping down behind her, wrapping around her waist and pulling her closer. Closer and closer until she couldn't tell where his heated body left off and hers began. She leaned into him, feeling the hard, fast pounding of his heart against hers. Finally responding to her lungs' demand for oxygen, she pulled back against the hand cradling her head, noting that Jake's arm was around her shoulder.

How many arms does the man have? she wondered in confusion. One was definitely wrapped around her waist. The other rested between her shoulder blades, with its hand testing the texture of her hair and the thumb stroking her earlobe, sending shivers through her body. And *another* was lying along her shoulders?

At that moment, Jake's cheek nuzzled against hers, slightly raspy even though he had shaved before dinner. "Honey, I know I got an abbreviated version of your life history earlier, but is there anything vital you forgot to tell me?"

"Like what?" she asked in bemusement.

"Like why you have a tail growing out of your ear?"

She blinked at him, wondering if she had heard correctly. He leaned back, and she realized that the raucous sound in her ear was not the result of overheated blood charging through her veins like a freight train, but Peg's purring. A supremely satisfied Peg, if the expression on his furry face was any indication.

Jake's tone was one of flat determination. "I'm going to kill me a cat," he announced. "Or haul him up on the roof and let him find his own way down. That should take at least a month." He stood up, reached for Shanda's hands and pulled her up beside him. His eyes gleaming with satisfaction, he watched Peg tumble to the cushions, then stalk away, muttering feline curses.

"Let's see," Jake muttered, turning her to face him, "I think we were just about here. . . ." He enclosed her once again in his arms and lowered his head, brushing her lips with his.

Shanda, you idiot, don't let him start! Being in his arms is like catching the flu. Your head rings, your muscles go weak and your mind slips into neutral. Get away from the man while you're still able to move!

Reluctantly following her own advice, Shanda pushed against Jake's shoulders. She didn't bother to shield her revealing eyes. He was experienced enough to know what he was doing to her. She merely shook her head slowly from side to side as he looked down at her.

"No?"

"No. If you want to sit over there"—she pointed to the leather chair—"while I sit here"—the same finger pointed to the sofa—"we can talk. Otherwise, I'll say good night."

"Ah, St. James, you're a hard nut to crack," he said as

he led her to the corner of the couch. She sat down. Holding one of her hands, he dropped into the nearby chair. "What do you want to talk about?"

"You're the one who hauled me in here. I was trying to go upstairs, remember?"

"You don't want to go sit in an empty room."

"I should be so lucky. There's always someone in it."

"Peg doesn't count. He's only a cat."

Shanda smiled. "Don't tell him that. He'd be awfully upset."

Jake's fingers tightened, warning her before the words were spoken. "I'm leaving in the morning. The sooner I go, the sooner I'll get this thing tied up for J.B. Can I count on finding you at the ranch when I get back?"

"Does it matter?"

"You damn well know it does!"

"Why?"

"Because we have some unfinished business to attend to. A lot of it."

"Jake, I don't know what you're up to—" She stopped abruptly at the knowing look in his eyes. "Erase that. I know *exactly* what you're up to and you might as well forget it. You want a bed partner for an indefinite period of time and you've decided that I'll fill the gap. Well, it's not going to happen. You might as well get out your little black book, personal computer or whatever you use and start going down your list."

"Why?" His quietly voiced question rattled her.

"Why what?"

"Why won't you go to bed with me?"

Damn and blast the man! Couldn't he just take his rejection and leave? No, that obviously wasn't his style.

He'd have to discuss it to death, worry it like a dog with a bone.

Taking a firm grip on her emotions, she settled back, trying and failing to release her hand from his warm grasp. Giving up on that, she took a steady breath before she spoke.

"You've held me in your arms, and you know exactly what you do to me when you kiss me. You scramble my thoughts and turn my brains to mashed potatoes. But I'll be damned if I'll go to bed with a man just to get him out of my system."

Goaded by his silence, she continued. "It may seem old-fashioned, but I grew up with parents who were crazy in love with each other. My father was the only man my mother ever looked at. I want something as rare and beautiful as that for myself."

Defiantly holding his steady gaze, she said, "I've waited this long and I'll survive a little longer. So, to answer your question, I'll be at the ranch when you get back, but I won't be there for you." She stood, only to find him on his feet next to her.

"You little idiot. Do you think I look at women as meals to be devoured and then forgotten?" He pulled her against him, plastering her to his hard length, kissing her until her tense body melted against his and her fingers laced through his black hair, kneading and caressing. He lifted his mouth, slowly brushed his lips across hers one last time and turned her toward the door.

"I'll be back as soon as I can. You be where I can find you."

Once again he watched her walk through a door, away from him—watched that erect back and those trim hips swaying in unconscious feminine seduction. Yes, by God, he'd be back and they'd just see how long she was willing to wait. His hand froze as he reached for the file. Wait for what? he wondered suddenly. An affair? She had just stated her position unequivocally. Gifted him with her honesty. Could he do that to her? Would he, even if he could?

Chapter Seven

Shanda was sitting on J.B.'s velvet lawn admiring his rambling, two-story ranch house when a car drove up.

"Barry! Am I glad to see you!" Shanda launched herself at the young man staggering under a burden of cameras and various bags laden with the rest of his paraphernalia.

"Stop!" he commanded, keeping her at arms' length. "Don't touch me until I get rid of this stuff." His long legs made quick work of the six porch steps and he shed his equipment with the loving care of a mother laying down her newborn. "Now," he said, turning with open arms, "you can hug me."

"Big, hairy deal," Shanda mumbled into his chest. "Here I was ready to give you a thousand-watt, spontaneous hug and you put me on hold. I bet you don't do that to Nora."

"Then you'd lose. She knows better than to attack me

when I'm carrying several thousand bucks' worth of equipment." He loosened his hold, looking around for a place to sit. Shanda led him to a cushioned porch swing and he collapsed next to her in a boneless sprawl, pushing back the straight brown hair that the wind had swept over his forehead.

"All right, woman, talk. I feel like someone in a James Bond movie who never got his script. You called me last night, talked for all of thirty seconds, told me to get my rear in gear, be at the airport at the crack of dawn and be prepared to shoot miles of film. I would be met, you said."

"Obviously, you were."

"Yeah. By a pair of cowboy boots and a Stetson separated by about five feet of skinny muscle. I was packed into a private plane, flown to Oklahoma City, led to a helicopter and brought here."

"So what more do you want?"

"A little information. The guy who brought me out here must be related to a clam. The conversation consisted of 'get in,' 'buckle up,' 'get out,' 'get in,' 'buckle up' and 'here we are.' "

He grinned reluctantly at her peal of laughter. "I'm not kidding, Shanda; I don't even know where I am."

"Poor Barry. Well, for starters, you're sitting on the front porch of the J. B. McCade ranch house."

"*The* J.B. McCade? The oil man?"

"See? You already know more than I did when I got here. I didn't know there was any *the* about it. I was just looking up a distant relative."

"Okay. So you have a good reason for being here. What's mine?"

She pointed to his pile of equipment. "That. But it's a

long story and I want you to get settled first. Have you eaten?''

He groaned pathetically. "Since when? I missed breakfast, and the pint-sized birdman scheduled a nonstop flight.''

"That settles it. I'm not talking until you get some food in you. Come on, I'll help you with this stuff.''

Barry followed hot on her heels through the door and up the stairs. He released an explosive sigh of relief as she opened a heavy oak door and stopped beside a queen-size bed.

"You're getting paranoid. You know that, don't you?'' Shanda demanded as she carefully placed her burden on the bed.

He eyed her balefully. "And who would be screaming bloody murder if something went wrong with my equipment and I couldn't get the shots you wanted, exactly when you wanted them?''

She grabbed his arm and hustled him to the door. "Food,'' she said resolutely. "Not one more word until you eat something. J.B. had to run some errands and he told me to play hostess. So my first act as lady of the manor will be to introduce you to Ruby.''

He looked a question at her.

"Ruby, as you'll soon learn, is one of the two best cooks in Oklahoma. Her sister, Gladys, is the other.''

Watching Ruby's portly, aproned figure bustle around, tsk-tsking as she placed a steaming plate in front of Barry, Shanda leaned back in her chair. She thought of the day before and realized once again that when the McCade men decided to do something, they *moved*. Jake had left for Texas and J.B. had shifted into high gear. He made a series of mysterious phone calls, advised Shanda to repack her clothes and asked her to corral Peg for the trip. The last task had been the easiest, for Peg rarely left her side.

At dinner Shanda had tried again. "Come on, J.B. At least give me a hint. This is driving me nuts!"

"One more day. Then you'll know."

"Does it have something to do with my film-making?"

He mulled over the question, then said, "Possibly."

Resting her chin in her open hand, she had coaxed, "Jake is gone now, so I can't possibly spill the beans. Come on, give." Watching his carefully blank face in exasperation, she bet herself that he had garnered a batch of his early oil wells in poker games.

Changing her approach, she had asked, "Would you ask me to do this if I didn't make films?"

"No." The answer came after a long, thoughtful silence. "It's a good thing I never had a daughter," he added grimly. "She would have had me wrapped around her finger before she was three. That's all you're getting out of me, so you'd better be satisfied."

She wasn't. She had sat quietly, thinking. He obviously wanted her to make a film of some sort for him. And, just as obviously, he didn't have the vaguest idea of the myriad tasks and details involved. Or the time. Or the fact that it wasn't a one-man operation.

Her voice had had a brisk, executive edge to it as she had pushed once again. "If this is leading where I think it is and the time limit's a short one, I'm going to need Barry Nolan—and fast." She answered the question implicit in his arched, heavy white brows. "Barry's my cameraman." After a long silence, she had asked her final question. "Do I need him?"

"Call him. Tonight. Tell him he'll be picked up at LAX in the morning."

Now, watching her friend gobble his food, Shanda could hardly wait for his reaction. She had had a busy morning with J.B., had finally learned what he wanted. He had taken her on a tour of the ranch, spending most of the time on a twenty-acre site located on the southwest corner of his property. Strolling around the area, pointing out first one section, then another, he had explained.

"But why all the secrecy?" Shanda had asked. "Why keep Jake in the dark?"

J.B. had grinned and Shanda could see the youthful spirit that still lurked within him. "A couple of years ago Jake and I built a museum for the town. Every year since, at the Buellton annual celebration, we've each donated something to it. I wouldn't admit this to anyone else, but it's gotten a mite competitive."

Substitute "dog-eat-dog" for "mite" and you'd be a lot closer to the truth, Shanda had thought with a grin.

"I want you to make a film about the early settlers—how they lived, how they settled the town, you know the sort of thing I mean. Something that will make the young people today proud of their heritage."

"Is that all?" Shanda had asked faintly. "And how long do I have for this little project?"

"About a month."

"A *month?* Do you have any idea—"

"No, but I have money. All you need. More than you need. To be used any way that will oil the wheels."

"I wish you'd quit talking about oil," Shanda had grumbled. "It's not the answer to everything."

"It helps, honey. It helps." He had leaned against a wooden fence, resting his forearms on the top rail. "You seem awfully young to be where you are in this business. How did you get started?"

"I followed in Aunt Paige's footsteps and enrolled in college as a history major. Social history intrigued me and I did my research on immigrants, immigration patterns and town settlements, using film analysis whenever possible. My interest in films led me to classes on film processing. I was involved in a doctoral program when I was asked to be an advisor for a documentary. The rest, as they say, is history. No pun intended. I was in the right place at the right time with the necessary knowledge and experience.''

"And you like it?"

"I love it. Can't imagine doing anything else.''

"What about the future? Marriage? A family?"

Her voice had been serious. "I want it all. I know what a good marriage can be and I won't settle for anything less. With the right man, there'll be room for my work, a family and anything else we want to fit in.''

"He wants us to *what?* Tell me you're kidding,'' Barry pleaded.

"All he wants,'' Shanda said with a straight face, "is an hour-long, Technicolor extravaganza wrapped up in a month. Now that's not asking much, is it?''

"Only a bloody miracle, that's all.''

Seeing his genuine concern, Shanda relented. "Wait till you see the setup he has, Barry. I think we can do it. He's turned part of the ranch into a restored town called Old Town, something like the one in San Diego. He's got everything from a sod house to the first hotel and, for a bonus, a train depot. And, get this, every year the people celebrate Pioneer Day. It's the city's birthday party. They dress up in old-time clothes and reenact the old days.''

She laughed softly. "J.B.'s out rallying the troops now.

Everybody's pulling out their costumes and getting ready. They're dying to be in a movie. So we have the location and a ready-made cast.''

"Who's going to handle the script, the narration, the music, the graphics, the—''

"J.B. doesn't know it yet, but he's our narrator.''

"An amateur?''

"You haven't met him yet. Just wait. As soon as he opens his mouth, you'll agree that he's perfect.''

"And what about the script? Who's going to write it?''

"That may be our miracle. Our first step is to haul down about fifteen boxes from the attic. It's all stuff that J.B.'s father collected over the years. I'm expecting to find some diaries in there. If we're in luck, with a bit of organizing and editing, they'll be the basis of our script.''

"I don't believe it,'' he said. "Nothing like that happens in the real world.''

"Then we're going to pretend we live in Disneyland because I don't have time to do the necessary research. Go get your grubbies on,'' she ordered. "We're about to attack the attic.''

An hour later, an imposing number of boxes and oddly shaped parcels were stored in a small room near Shanda's bedroom. "No, don't put that one down,'' Shanda directed. "J.B. had a table and chair brought up so I could work in here, but I think I'd rather have one box at a time in my bedroom. I just hope that a family of mice haven't set up housekeeping in there.''

Barry jiggled the box impatiently. "This thing weighs a ton. Show me where you want it before my back gives out. I have a nasty feeling I'm not covered by worker's comp on this job.''

"My hero," Shanda murmured as she opened her door and pointed to a spot near a comfortable chair.

"If you wanted a hero, you should have kept Lee around."

"Rats! Missed my chance again." She eyed Barry's lanky six feet. "But then Lee doesn't know anything about the working end of a camera, so I guess I'm still ahead."

Prodding the twine-tied box with the toe of her sandal, Shanda fought the impulse to open the box and dig through its contents. Instead, she turned once again to Barry.

"I wonder if Nora knows how sexy you are with cobwebs hanging off your eyebrows." She laughed as he glanced in the mirror.

"I notice that you managed to stay clean."

"Of course," she replied. "We established a long time ago that I'm the brains and you're the brawn of this outfit. Why do you think I wanted you to go first?"

He peeled off a sticky cobweb and dangled it threateningly over her head, twisting an imaginary moustache with his other hand. "Now, me proud beauty," he said, cackling, "I have you just where I want you."

"No!" she shrieked, flinging out a hand dramatically and jumping aside to avoid the sticky mess. "Not that! Oh, will no one save me from this dastardly deed?"

"Do we need the Texas Rangers or can a lone cowboy do the job?" J.B. inquired drily from the open doorway.

"To the rescue, and just in the nick of time!" Shanda crowed, throwing her arms around the older man's neck and kissing him noisily on the chin. Ignoring the sudden flush on his cheeks, she said, "J.B., although he looks

like an escapee from a horror flick, this is Barry Nolan,
the man who's going to create some magic for you.''

Later that evening, Shanda was sitting cross-legged on
the floor of her bedroom. Smiling, she thought of the two
men downstairs, interrupting each other as they examined
a map of the restored town. J.B. explained as Barry asked
one pertinent question after another. She and J.B. had
already discussed the major points. They didn't need her
right now.

The two men would work well together. After one
searching glance, they had reached out to shake hands,
Barry ruefully brushing his dirty hand across the seat of
his dusty jeans first. There had been an instant acceptance,
each man acknowledging the expertise of the other in his
own field. Yes, she decided, it was best to leave them
together for a while.

And I can get on with this, she thought in satisfaction.
This, of course, was the large box sitting in front of her.
The twine proved to be tough. It wouldn't break or stretch
enough so that she could pull it off one corner. Lacking
scissors and too impatient to run down to the kitchen for a
knife, she was soon hacking at it with a metal fingernail
file. The surge of pleasure she felt when the ragged ends of
the string split soon dissipated. The box was full of old
ledgers. Probably invaluable for Aunt Paige's purposes,
but she'd have to check them out later. Right now she
needed diaries.

Shoving the bulky carton against the wall, she went into
the next room and returned with a smaller one. Dropping
back down on the floor, she hesitated, looking at her
hands. With a grimace, she got up. Five minutes later she
was back with a pair of utility scissors and a cutter with a
straight-edged razor blade. She didn't consider herself a

vain person, but there was no sense in making a jagged mess of her fingernails. Also, if she was going to be continually switching boxes around, she decided, a small dolly would be handy. She made a mental note to ask J.B. for one.

"This isn't going to work," she muttered in disgust a few seconds later, peering at the contents of the second box. There was a miscellaneous collection of papers, a few photos and more ledgers. "Every blasted box is going to have to be opened and organized." So much for finding the diaries on the first attempt. Or the second. She felt a sudden sense of urgency. Having committed herself to the project, she was now as anxious as J.B. to have it finished for the opening celebration.

Grabbing a pencil and pad, she scribbled a few notes. First, get a firm date from J.B. His vague "about a month" was not enough. Next, find and edit the diaries so that she could get the shooting script and the scene breakdown written. Lordy, that was almost a month's work right there! She sincerely hoped that three cantankerous old men would keep Jake on the run for the next four weeks.

Just then the telephone sounded and she knew whose voice she would hear before she lifted the receiver. "Hello."

"Shanda?"

"Yes." Idiot. Who else did he expect?

"*The* Shanda St. James? Rising star in the world of television documentaries?"

"The one and only." Her tone became accusing. "You've been snooping, haven't you?"

"I have to," he said grimly. "*You* won't tell my anything."

"Because you never asked. You reach out, grab some half-witted idea, then toss accusations around as if they were confetti. If you want to know something about me, all you have to do is ask and be willing to listen. Why on earth did you bother calling?" she demanded in exasperation. "We haven't been talking two minutes and already we're arguing."

"Because I miss you like hell and I wanted to hear the sound of your voice."

"Oh."

"Well?"

"Well, what?"

"Do you miss me?"

Lord, yes, she missed him. He had taken all the light and color and excitement with him and she hadn't even realized it until now. But she didn't want to. He was arrogant, pigheaded and too rich for his own good. She didn't need a man like that in her life.

"I asked you a question." She could visualize his stubborn, wide-legged stance and knew he'd be on the phone all night, if necessary, waiting for an answer.

"I suppose so," she admitted grudgingly.

"Lady, you are something else." She flinched as he bit off the words. "Money doesn't impress you, power doesn't impress you and I don't impress you. Just what the hell are you looking for in a man?"

"Someone who will love me just as I am, warts and all. What I'm *not* looking for is a tomcat who sees a woman and automatically prepares to bed her. Any more questions?"

"Do you have warts?"

"No." She grinned at his bland tone but kept her voice

level. "A mole," she admitted, being scrupulously honest.

"Hold on a minute."

She heard a rustling sound at the other end of the line. "What are you doing?"

"I'm writing myself a note to cultivate an interest in moles."

"Will you stop it! You know what I mean."

"Where is it?"

His abrupt question drove the smile from her face. She remembered how his dark eyes had gleamed as they had lingered on her breasts, her waist and her hips that day at the pool. Never before had a man made her so uncomfortably aware of the shape of her own body. Never before had she responded so primitively to a silent male invitation. True, the response had been internal, reluctant and unacted upon. But it had been there. And they both knew it.

"Forget it," she advised, sorry she had even mentioned it. Changing the subject abruptly, she asked, "How's the search going? Are you hot on the trail of Mr. Cole, Perkins or Jurgens?"

"I'm in Dallas after Perkins. I hope to corral him tomorrow and then go on to Austin. I hope to God I can wind this thing up in a couple of days. What are you doing?"

"Lolling on the veranda drinking mint juleps."

His chuckle was a warm, masculine sound. "Wrong part of the country. Try again."

"Actually, I'm keeping busy." An understatement if there ever was one, she thought wryly. "Since you know my dark secret, I'll confess. My next documentary is on the Southwest—the opening of the Indian territories, the run into Oklahoma, that kind of stuff. My original purpose in vacationing in this part of the country was to look the area over."

Barry walked by at that moment, glanced in her open door and waved a casual good night.

" 'Night, Barry." Shanda waved absently.

"Who was that?" The brusk question sounded coldly in her ear.

"Barry Nolan, my cameraman, a genius, and my best friend."

"The one who called at the hotel the other night?"

"Uh-huh."

"The one you share?"

The sarcastic question ignited her temper. I will not lose control and scream at him like a fishwife, she told herself. I will keep my temper even if it kills me. "Barry is my friend," she said clearly. "His wife, Nora, is also my friend. Their little boy is my godson." Her voice soared on the last word and he held the telephone away from his ear, wincing.

"Oh." He'd done it again, he thought, closing his eyes in frustration. Why did he always say the wrong thing to this woman? Why, in God's name, did he interpret everything she said in the worst possible way?

"Oh?" he heard her say coldly. "Is that another famous McCade nonapology?"

He was angry and it could be heard in his voice. "No, it was a prelude to an apology. As in 'Oh, I'm sorry I shot off my big mouth.' "

"Oh."

He paced as far as the telephone cord would allow

before he continued. "Shanda, I'm sorry. I doubt if you'll believe this, but I'm usually fairly easy-going. I haven't been with you and I'm sorry."

"Well," she said in amazement, "when you finally get around to apologizing, you go all out, don't you? Can we be friends now?"

"Friendship isn't exactly what I have in mind. But I'm too far away for anything else, so, for now, I'll settle for that."

Her sigh of relief came through loud and clear. "Good," she said, responding to the latter part of his comment and ignoring the rest. "Now that that's settled, do you want to hear what I've been up to?"

He sat in a chair which was too small for his body, shifted uncomfortably and crossed his booted feet on the coffee table. "Uh-huh. Every single thing. I want to know what to expect when I get home."

"I feel in love with Old Town," she said, crossing her fingers and telling herself it wasn't *that* much of a lie, "and I called Barry down to get some shots. It's going at everything backwards since my new documentary script isn't even written, but we've worked together so long that we'll be able to make most of it work. The people in town are pulling out their old-time clothes and will help us with some scenes. So don't be surprised if it looks like a three-ring circus when you get back."

"J.B.'s probably in his glory," he said, amused. Then his voice deepened without warning. "But what about you, Shanda. When the work is over and you're in your room, alone in the dark. Are you lonely? Do you want a man beside you? Do you want me?"

"Jake, for heaven's sake!"

"I want you," he said simply. "I want to undress you, to touch you, to make you feel things you've never even imagined."

"Jake!"

"Tell me one thing, Shanda."

"What?"

"Right this very minute, is your body aching the way mine is?"

"Damn you, Jake McCade," she answered in a shaken whisper. "Yes, it is. But I'll get over it."

"Like hell you will, lady. There's no way on earth you'll get rid of that ache without me."

He expected no response and got none. There was only a soft click, followed by a dial tone. Frowning, he slowly replaced the receiver.

A long time later, he was still sitting in the undersized chair, staring at the telephone. His life was fine just as it was, he assured himself irritably. Just fine. He didn't lack for women. They were all around him. Blondes, redheads, brunettes; tall, petite, slim—whatever he wanted. So why was he sitting here thinking of a chestnut-haired, blue-eyed witch with a dazzling smile and a nasty temper? His mind flicked momentarily to Janell, the tall, cool blonde with hot, black eyes. Why wasn't he returning her call? His black eyes glittered in anger when he couldn't answer his own question.

Chapter Eight

"My God, girl, what are you doing to yourself? Your eyes look like two burnt holes in a blanket!" The concerned look on J.B.'s face matched his tone as he looked at her across the breakfast table.

Shanda yawned and ran a weary hand through her hair, pushing it behind her ear. It was her fourth day on the ranch and she was exhausted. The diaries had been found. She had arranged them in chronological order and read them until her eyes rebelled. It didn't take long for them to reach that state because Buell, although surprisingly loquacious, was not a man of letters. His spelling was highly original and his writing was an annoying combination of squiggles and scrawls.

Once she had broken his code her reading went a bit faster, but she still had to contend with dull pencil marks that faded away and splotches of ink. She had spent precious minutes frowning over a staggered series of ink dots. Finally, she had decided that a bug had fallen into an inkblot and stamped around the paper until its feet were clean.

When her eyes cried for mercy, she walked around mumbling to herself, assimilating what she had read. In her excitement, she had neither noted J.B.'s puzzled look of inquiry nor heard Barry's explanation that this was normal gestation behavior for her.

The material was fantastic! Although he wrote in a detached style, Buell had a remarkable eye for color and detail. His description of the "Run of '89," when thousands of eager settlers raced into newly opened land to claim farms and town sites, was breathtaking. Her fingers itched to get it all on paper. J.B. was going to be pleased, she thought in the understatement of the year. Buell's books were a rich historical legacy. As well as supplying information for the film, they could be transcribed and reprinted, and would make a priceless addition to the museum.

J.B.'s voice brought her back to the present. "Are you listening to me, Shanda? I said you look like the wrath of God. What've you been doing to yourself? You're supposed to be on vacation."

She looked up to catch his worried glance. "I'm also here to do a film for you, remember? One with a deadline that only a madman would consider acceptable. It can't get off the ground without a script and I can't write one until I read the material. But I'll have the reading finished in another day or so and I'm already starting the script. So, not to worry, love."

"I'm not nearly as concerned about that as I am about

the way you look," he grumbled. "At least get out in the sun today."

"And the wind. Just as a matter of interest, does it ever stop? Yesterday, I asked one of your men if the wind always blows this way. He just looked poker-faced and said, 'No, sometimes it blows *that* way.'"

J.B. grinned. "You walked into one of the oldest jokes in Oklahoma." He set his coffee cup down. "But I want you out of this house for a few hours, away from those books." She agreed so meekly that he eyed her suspiciously.

"Actually, I was going to ask if I could borrow a pickup to drive out to Old Town." Barry looked up from his plate full of pancakes. "No, I don't need you. I want some time down there by myself."

An hour later, she was on her way, with Peg curled up beside her on the seat. Yawning again, she admitted to herself that she was indeed tired, but the long hours spent on the diaries weren't the only reason. Jake's nightly telephone calls, his deep voice and outrageous comments, resulted in restless churning during the hours when she should have been deeply asleep. He was getting to her and she suspected that he knew it.

What was she going to do about him? she wondered, her hands steady on the steering wheel as the truck bumped over the rutted dirt road, leaving a spiral of red dust stretched out behind it. She had known him less than two weeks and he made no secret of his intentions. He wanted her slender body in his king-size bed. The sooner, the better.

Against her will, she found herself wondering what it would be like. Unless she planned to go to her grave unwed and depressingly chaste, there had to be a first time. Why not him? He certainly had the experience to make it pleasurable! She responded to him physically in a way that still managed to shock and surprise her. And he could be fun. It was important, she told herself seriously, that he had a sense of humor.

All in all, she decided gloomily, he would be fantastic. For as long as it lasted. And then what? He would go on to another woman, and she would . . . That was a good question. What would she do? Find out that she was a one-man woman and languish away like some Victorian maiden? Or—or nothing, she vowed. That was the same kind of empty-headed thinking that got her engaged to Lee. She wasn't so desperate that she'd fall into the arms of the nearest man, even if he was devastating.

After parking the truck in the shade of a large, craggy oak tree, she jumped down and walked over to the first of the old buildings. Peg ambled along beside her, then, apparently impatient with her slow pace, struck off on his own.

Perched comfortably on a split-rail fence, Shanda examined the sod house, recalling Buell's description of constructing one. It sounded deceptively simple. They had used a plow to turn the ground up five or six inches. Sod pieces were cut into strips about a yard long and piled on top of each other as if they were bricks. Water between the strips cemented them together. When the walls were complete, lumber or boughs were added for a roof, with more strips of sod on top. Once a door and windows were added, the job was complete. Many farmers had settled in such homes, putting aside their dreams of a clapboard house until they were more prosperous. Many had never made it.

Shanda moved on to a log cabin consisting of two rooms with dirt floors and an open breezeway between them. A little farther down, a two-story clapboard house was tucked into a curve in the road and a large, pillared, white antebellum mansion sat on a grassy knoll. She stood before each one, mentally seeing it through Barry's lens, fitting it neatly into the developing script. A tingle of excitement worked its way down her spine. Not only would it work, it would be good, damn good!

Dropping down in the shade of a pecan tree, she stretched out, cupping her hands beneath her head. Looking past the green leaves to the blue sky beyond, she breathed rhythmically, willing the tension from her body. She had done her homework, and experience had taught her that even if she slept, her subconscious would be on the job. She would awake with her muddled thoughts all neatly assembled in a tidy package, ready to go.

Lord, but it felt good to lie there. The warm grass pricked through her thin cotton shirt in a familiar, comfortable way. A bee buzzed nearby in the clover and she hoped lazily that she wasn't intruding on its territory. The hot, dry smell of grass and newly turned earth was almost intoxicating. Her contentment went deeper as the silence became more obvious. No distant sound of cars, no voices, not even the rustle of leaves. For once, it seemed, even the ever-present wind had died. On that comfortable thought, she slept.

"Shanda. Get your butt down here. On the double!"

Blinking, she jerked up to a sitting position, her eyes losing their sleep-dazed expression and growing brilliant with irritation. There was only one man she knew who would be so rude, but this was going some, even for him. The rapid thud of booted feet brought her upright.

"Just who do you think you're talking to, Jake Mc-Cade?" But before the last word had been uttered, she knew something was desperately wrong. "J.B.?" she gasped.

"He's fine. Come on, we've got to get out of here," he insisted, hauling her behind him to the truck parked next to hers.

"Just a damned minute! You come up here yelling like a banshee and I'm supposed to meekly—"

He brought an end to her heated words by clapping his hands on her shoulders and turning her so that her back was to him. He clamped her to his chest with one brawny arm while he pointed the other straight ahead. "What do you see out there?"

"Where?" she asked in confusion.

"There!"

"Just some clouds." Then she squinted and said hesitantly, "Funny-looking clouds. One of them looks like the bottom dropped out." The next words came slowly, painfully. "Oh, my God. Jake, is it a—"

"Tornado," he said flatly. "About a mile away and coming fast. Come on," he added, "we've got to get out of here." He tossed her up on the seat, snapped, "Buckle up," and loped around to the other side.

"Peg! We can't leave without him."

Jake looked down at her as if she had lost her senses. "If you think I'm risking our lives for a cat—"

The discussion was immaterial because, at that moment, Peg launched himself through the open window like a torpedo. Landing with all the grace of an upended crate of tomatoes, he whizzed past Shanda, slid onto the center section of the bench seat and ended up tangled between Jake and the steering wheel. Before he could regain his lost dignity, Jake tossed him onto Shanda's lap with the terse order, "Hang on to him."

"What are you going to do?" She watched as he shifted gears and pushed on the gas pedal.

"Outrun it."

Casting a nervous look over her shoulder and then at the speedometer, she asked, "How fast do you have to go?"

"Don't know. Never had to do it." His grin was a white flash against his dark skin as he turned to her. "Exactly where is it in relation to us?"

"Right behind us," she said in a small voice, wondering if she would ever understand men. He was actually *smiling*.

"Hang on, then. I'm turning left up here."

She followed orders, hanging on to whatever was available. At least the seat belt kept her from sliding into Jake, she thought with relief. The last thing she wanted to do was distract him, especially with the speedometer needle hovering on one hundred and ten.

"Where is it now?"

"It switched too. It's running parallel with us."

"How far away?"

"I don't know," she said, almost frozen with fear. "Too close for comfort."

He took a quick glance. "It's almost a quarter of a mile away. Not too bad."

"My God, it just ate a tree!"

"Better it than us. Hold on. I'm turning left again."

"It's going on! You did it, Jake, you did it!"

"Don't plan a party for a few minutes. Those things jump around like grasshoppers."

Their circular route had brought them back to where her truck was parked and she noted with relief that Old Town had suffered no damage. They climbed down and watched the gray funnel touch down on an old barn about half a mile away. Jake handed her a pair of binoculars. It was like watching an old silent film, she thought. Sections of the roof were lifted and engulfed. One wall sailed away like a Frisbee and the others just exploded, rotting boards tossed in all directions.

She heaved a sigh of relief and handed him the binoculars. "Thanks. For those and the rescue. How on earth did you arrive just in the nick of time?" she asked, hoping to distract him. Now that they were out of danger, she could see the anger beneath his calm just waiting for an outlet.

"Will you tell me," he said so quietly that she flinched, "just what the hell you were doing out here on your own?"

"I *am* over twenty-one," she reminded him. "I don't need a keeper."

"You couldn't prove it by me. Why didn't you at least have the radio on?"

"I was thinking," she retorted loftily, stung by his comment. "I don't normally have the radio blaring when I'm concentrating on something."

"Out here, at this time of the year, you can't afford to forget the weather. Ever." The anger had drained from his voice and now she noted only his weariness.

Remorse filled her. "Oh, Jake, I'm sorry." She moved closer, wrapping her arms around his waist and resting her head near his shoulder. "Thank you for coming after me. I really do appreciate it. I didn't mean to snarl at you. You look so tired, too. What on earth have you been doing to yourself?"

He wrapped his arms around her and pulled her closer. "Chasing old men."

"How shocking," she said, giggling.

"Brat," he responded, tugging lightly at her hair so that he could see her face. A frown etched his forehead as he touched the mauve shadows beneath her eyes. "What about these?" he demanded.

"I have a perfectly logical explanation." Innocent blue eyes met demanding dark ones. "Late every night I get a kinky call from someone who makes the most indecent suggestions. I thought I was being hounded because of my youth and beauty, but I recently learned that he really has a thing for the geriatric set, and male at that, and—"

"Shut up, you little idiot." His face blotted out the sunlight and warm lips covered hers as she closed her eyes. The kiss was neither gentle nor searching. It was an outright statement of possession, she realized. That one fleeting thought was all she was capable of. Her lips parted beneath his as his hands drew her ever closer until her body molded itself to every hard plane of his. When they came up for air, she was slumped against him, her fingers twined in his hair.

His chest rose as he filled his lungs with a deep, unsteady breath. He slid his hands down until they fitted snugly in the back pockets of her jeans and drew her even closer. He watched as the dazed passion in her eyes was replaced by shocked awareness of his state of arousal. She instinctively arched her back in an attempt to retreat, then flushed as the movement only brought her closer to him. She dropped her hands to his shoulders and pushed.

"Jake, don't . . . please."

With obvious reluctance, he released her. "Someday,

lady mine, it will be the right time and place for us. But it won't be on the ground or in the back of a truck. And," he added, with a wary look at Peg, who was eyeing him unblinkingly, "it won't be where that cat can sharpen his claws on my backside."

He took her hand and led her to the trucks. "Come on, I'll follow you back to the ranch."

Shanda climbed into J.B.'s truck and started the ignition. A few minutes later she glanced back through the rearview mirror. Jake had given her a head start so that he wouldn't be eating her dust and she could barely make out his truck. Good lord, but the man had a potent charm! She lifted one hand from the steering wheel and frowned as it trembled. Charm was not the word, she decided. Raw sexuality was more like it. No, not that either. Sexuality? Absolutely. But raw? No way.

As she circled the house, she noticed Barry, with his video camera and tripod, and J.B. standing on the lawn deep in conversation. After she had parked and gotten out of the truck, she dashed around to the front yard.

"Did you get it?" she asked.

Barry stepped well away from the camera and turned to her with a exultant grin. "Baby, you'd better have a spot for one mean twister in that script because I've got stuff that will knock your socks off!"

"Whoopee! I knew you'd do it!" Shanda almost strangled him when she threw her arms around his neck. He picked her up and whirled her around as J.B. looked on indulgently. Their mutual celebration ground to an abrupt halt as a truck door slammed.

"Do you know someone who looks like the Incredible Hulk with indigestion and a nasty temper?" he asked nervously. After another quick glance, he added, "And seems to think you should be enclosed in a fence posted 'Private Property'?"

"Ah, Jake must be here," she said blithely and heard J.B.'s sudden chuckle turn into a frenzied cough.

She turned and, wrapping an arm around Barry's waist, leaned against him. Watching the angry man approach, his heels gouging holes in the manicured lawn, she thought that Barry's description was remarkably accurate. When he was three steps away, she made her move.

"Jake, I want you to meet my friend, Barry Nolan. We were just discussing the film footage he got of the tornado."

The look in her eye and the challenge of her smile stopped him in his tracks. She looked like a she-bear protecting her cub, Jake thought in sudden amusement. At the quizzical look on the face of the other man, he relaxed.

"Nolan," he acknowledged, extending his hand. "I've heard all about you from Shanda." He reached out, plucked her away from Barry, proprietarily tucked her into the curve of his arm and continued blandly. "Any friend of hers is automatically a friend of mine."

At dinner that evening, Shanda watched Jake with caution. He was affable and altogether too charming. He had, in effect, tossed down the gauntlet that afternoon and she was not one to refuse a challenge. But she was not foolhardy either. Be patient, she advised herself, returning his smile. Your time will come.

Jake's eyes lit with amusement as he watched the frustrated wrath gathering in Shanda's eyes. He wondered if she knew how expressive her face was. With Las Vegas so nearby, he hoped she wasn't fond of gambling.

"By the way," Shanda asked during the next conversational lull, "how did you happen to be around this afternoon to rescue me?"

J.B. spoke up. "Jake walked in just as the tornado watch was announced on the radio and got worried when he heard you were out alone."

"She was sleeping on the grass by the big house. Right in its path. I woke her up," Jake explained briefly to the other men.

"Yes, indeed," Shanda agreed drily. "His method left something to be desired, but it was effective. What I really meant, though"—she directed a look at Jake—"is why were you here at all? Did you get all the signatures you needed?"

"I caught up with Perkins in San Antonio." He cast a puzzled look at J.B. "If I didn't know better, I'd think he was avoiding me. I just missed him three days in a row. But his papers are signed and in your room. I'll stay for the weekend and take off Monday after the other two. I hope to hell they're settled in one place."

"Then you'll be here for the party," J.B. said. "Good."

"What party?" Their voices merged as three pair of eyes turned in his direction.

"The barbeque on Sunday. Didn't I mention it?" he asked, looking at each one in turn. "Well," he said in mild surprise as he saw three heads shake negatively, "I've invited some people from town to come and meet Shanda."

When Sunday arrived, there was no doubt in Shanda's mind that the entire town of Buellton was at the barbeque. J.B. monopolized Shanda, ignoring Jake's dark frown and spent the afternoon steering her from one group to another, introducing her as a cousin. "I'm not about to go into this 'great-granduncle' business," he told her in an aside. "Anyway, everyone around here understands cousins."

After she had made the official rounds, she gravitated to the older people. She had learned long ago that they were the ones with the information and the stories. She sat next to a plump, pink-faced woman with curly gray hair. "Nell, may I join you for a while?"

A wide smile and a pat on the hand welcomed her. "Of course, honey. Sit." Within minutes Shanda was surrounded by a ring of wrinkled, friendly faces and dazed by her good fortune. Nell, never one to subdue her curiosity, had learned in less than thirty seconds of Aunt Paige's search for family information. As fate would have it, she was a member of the local genealogical society and soon had the rest of the group clustered around. Shanda was inundated with invitations to view family pedigree charts and photo albums. After clarifying that Buell was the common ancestor she was following, the group invited her to their monthly meeting on the following Wednesday morning at the town library. Buell's relatives promised to make copies of their charts for her to send to Paige.

Shanda walked away from them, grinning. Aunt Paige would have the time of her life with that group.

A large hand on her bare arm stopped her. Jake's warm breath stirred her hair. "There's cream on your whiskers again, honey. What've you been up to now?"

"You know that gold mine I told you about? Well, I just fell smack dab into the middle of it. Those ladies"—she indicated the group with a tilt of her head—"are the Buellton Genealogical Society and they've just saved me months of searching through microfilms and dusty records.''

"Terrific. Now are you ready to eat?''

"I thought you'd never ask. The combination of hickory smoke and barbequed spare ribs is driving me crazy.''

"Good. You'll need your strength.''

"What do you mean?'' She looked up at him suspiciously.

"Not what you're thinking, unfortunately. Ed brought his fiddle and the caller's getting ready.''

"What on earth are you talking about?''

"Square dancing.''

"Oh, good. I love to watch it.''

"Tonight you're the guest of honor. You'll be *doing* it.''

"What? I don't know the first thing about it.''

"They'll be happy to teach you.''

"What do you mean, they? What'll you be doing?''

"Watching. I hate square dancing.''

Later, as he led her over to a group, she muttered, "I'll get you for this." And she might have tried if she hadn't so thoroughly enjoyed herself. As she swung, curtsied and sashayed, she laughed with her partners and pretended that dark eyes weren't following her every move.

Chapter Nine

It wasn't until a week later that Shanda opened the last of the cartons. Once the diaries had been found, she had concentrated on them. Anyway, she thought, shaking a sturdily wrapped rectangular box, this one was much too light to contain books. Snipping the knotted string, she tore off the paper and removed the lid. A faint scent of lavender drifted up from the silk pouches of sachet that lined the box. Her eyes rounded in amazed delight as she stared down at a mass of embroidered organdy, white on white. It was a wedding dress.

Standing, she lifted it by the shoulders and walked over to the full-length mirror. Supporting the fabric at the waist, she held it to her. Her face grew dreamy as she looked at her reflection. The dress had a deep square neck with tiny covered buttons down the front to below the waist. Full sleeves ended in deep buttoned cuffs. The floating skirt was full, with just a hint of a train, and the hem barely touched the floor.

Placing it gently on the bed, Shanda turned back to the box. She picked up a white, boned petticoat, strapless and full-length. The veil was a fingertip concoction of airy lace. Interesting, she thought, as well as beautiful. The dress was at least forty years old and must have raised a few eyebrows in its day. And the lady who wore it, she decided with admiration, had chutzpah.

Without wasting another moment, she tore off her shorts and blouse and stepped into the shower. When she had dried herself, she slipped into panty hose and high-heeled sandals. Some minutes later, she stood in front of the mirror securing the last button. It fit, but just barely. The waist was a bit snug and the bust a little loose. Yes, indeed, it had been *some* lady. She reached for the veil.

"Shanda?" J.B. called from the hall as he knocked on the unlatched door.

"Come in."

"I just finished another tape and thought you'd want to put it with the—My God!" At the stunned whisper, she whirled to face him, the skirt billowing and settling softly on the floor.

Shocked at the naked pain on his face, she reached out to the gallant old man she had learned to love. Her voice was urgent. "What's the matter, J.B.?"

He straightened and managed a crooked smile. But his eyes, those bright blue eyes, were clouded with emotion.

"Nothing, honey. You just . . . took me by surprise."

She suddenly knew and could hardly speak over the tightening of her throat. "It's your wife's dress, isn't it?"

"Yes. It's my Jenny's," he said simply.

Her voice was thick with distress. "Oh, J.B., I'm so

sorry. I wouldn't hurt you for the world and look what I've done.'' She blinked back tears as he lifted her hands to his face and placed one on each cheek.

He cleared his throat. "You're a lot like her," he said steadily. "A real hell raiser, but soft as a morning in May. You even look a bit like her, except her eyes were brown. Big, almond-shaped and beautiful as all outdoors.''

"She must have been very special.'' Shanda's thumbs lightly caressed his tan, leathery cheek, letting her touch convey what words could not.

"I had her for twenty-two years.'' The words were a heart-wrenching blend of gratitude and loneliness.

"Did you ever argue?'' she asked, thinking of Jake.

He chuckled. "We were both stubborn and hot-tempered. You bet we did. But we had a helluva time making up.'' He changed the subject abruptly. "Do you like the dress?''

"It's the loveliest thing I've ever seen.''

"I remember when she packed it away. Said it was going to be for our daughter. Hoped she'd want to get married in it. But we didn't have any children. We couldn't. A lot of years passed before we gave up hope. Even after we adopted Jake, we thought there still might be a chance. He filled the empty spot in our hearts, though. He was Jenny's sister's boy. His parents drowned the summer he was two. Then he was ours.''

Shanda stood quietly, looking at the top button of his shirt, letting him talk. He had never mentioned his marriage and now she knew why. His Jenny was wrapped away with special memories, not to be lightly shared.

He cleared his throat again, this time uneasily. "Anyway, I was wondering if you'd like the dress.''

The veil rustled as she looked up at him. Her eyes grew

misty and she spoke with difficulty. Clasping his hand, she said, "I've never been offered anything as beautiful. But I can't take something that's so precious to you."

His eyes were once again bright blue. "You're the closest I've come to having a daughter. Jenny and I would be pleased if you'd wear the dress at your wedding and keep it for your little girl."

After a long, emotion-charged silence, she lifted the veil and stood on her toes to kiss his cheek. "I'll consider it an honor."

"Good." He moved away, walking briskly to the door, then stopped and turned back to her. "Would you do something for me before you take it off?"

"For you, anything." Her attempt at lightness failed miserably.

"We were married in this house. I remember how Jenny walked down the stairs and, as she reached the last step, she stopped, smiled and held out her hand to me. I don't have any pictures. Never needed any. But I'd give a lot to see that one more time."

Slowly, she replaced the veil. "See you in a couple of minutes," she said softly. The door closed behind him.

Closing her eyes, she took a couple of steadying breaths. Shanda, she lectured herself sternly, you are going to meet that magnificent man with a smile so dazzling that it will knock him for a loop. And you are *not* going to cry!

Standing silently at the top of the stairs, she waited until he looked up. She was aware of a startled movement at the living room door, but her eyes were locked on J.B. His gaze met hers and his hand twitched involuntarily. She glided down the stairs, imagining how she would feel if she were going to meet the man she loved. Pausing at the bottom step, she smiled radiantly and reached out to J.B. His hand touched hers and she stepped forward. Her eyes slowly clouded with tears and she pressed her face against his chest, shutting out the sight of two damp paths slowly coursing down his cheeks.

"What the devil is going on here?" Jake's voice, oddly shaken, stopped her tears but only momentarily. If they had to come, at least let it be in the privacy of her room, she prayed silently. Gathering her skirt in her hands, she whirled, darted up the stairs to safety and left the explanations to J.B.

Several hours later Shanda was looking for Barry and J.B. She finally found them on the front porch, looking as if they had just solved the world's problems.

"You two are really something else. I've been slaving over storyboards and you're sitting here lapping up beer and sunshine."

Barry opened a reproachful eye. "Hush! We're testing a theory. And don't look so skeptical. It'll probably advance meteorology ten years. Come on, sit down and I'll tell you all about it."

"I can hardly wait."

He reached out and pulled a chair next to his. "See, J.B. says if you sit out here with your feet propped up on the porch rail watching the sky, there won't be a rainstorm." He looked at her expectantly.

"That's it?" She had the feeling she had missed something.

"That's it."

"And where does the beer come in?"

"That helps us stay out here longer."

"Keeping the rain away."

"Right."

"For your information, there isn't a cloud in the sky."

"What have I been telling you?" Barry asked in mock exasperation. "It works!"

J.B. pushed up the Stetson that had been shielding his eyes—eyes that now glimmered with amusement. "Of course, we haven't worked all the wrinkles out yet. We've only been at it a couple of hours."

"Idiots! Both of you." Smiling at J.B., she asked, "Why isn't Jake out here helping you? Doesn't he believe in your theory?"

"He's gone," J.B. replied, settling his hat over his eyes again. "He dropped off the Cole papers, and I thought he'd stay a while. But he had a bee in his bonnet, said he had to get going. Seemed upset about something."

"Oh," she said in a hollow voice. She had a pretty good idea what that "something" was. He probably thought she was poking around in J.B.'s belongings and didn't like the idea one bit. He probably also blamed her for upsetting J.B. earlier. She was surprised that he hadn't stayed long enough to tell her so. Sighing philosophically, she decided that she'd soon be hearing from him.

"Come on, you guys. We've got work to do." Ignoring Barry's groan, she passed him the storyboards. "These are the sketches I've done so far. A lot of the stuff you've already shot will work. You'll have to check to see if you need anything else. I'll have some more ready later tonight."

Barry looked them over, reading the description of each scene carefully. Seeing that he was already immersed in the material, Shanda moved over by J.B. She thought about how excited he had been when she had asked him to narrate the film. Here he was, a man who could go anywhere, do anything, buy anything he wanted, and he was as pleased as a kid with his first bike.

"Here's the first part of the script. Look it over, practice reading out loud and when you're satisfied, we'll try taping it."

"Yes, ma'am," he mumbled from beneath his hat.

She tipped the brim up with her finger and grinned at him. "Don't ma'am me, smarty. I've been known to fire narrators for less than that."

"These look pretty good," Barry interrupted. "I can adapt a lot of the footage—"

"Hey," J.B. said in a pleased tone, "you're starting off with me in the film."

"I thought we'd keep it in the family," Shanda said, smiling at the surprised look on his face. "I'm aiming for the intimate touch so I want to start with you talking about your father, do a flashback and then follow Buell's diary. At the end, we'll come back to you again."

"Well, I'll be—" he broke off, speechless.

Shanda bit back a grin. Apparently even an oil baron could be stagestruck.

"How do you want to start out, J.B.?" Barry asked. "You could charge over the top of a hill on your trusty steed, slide to a halt and start talking. Or you could climb down from the top of an oil well and when you hit bottom—"

"When this idiot runs down, maybe we can discuss it rationally," Shanda said drily.

J.B. looked out over the rolling green hills thoughtfully. "Even though he's sort of hare-brained," he said, tilting his head at Barry, "maybe he's on the right track."

"Nobody ever appreciates a genius," Barry mourned.

"Down, genius," Shanda ordered. "Let the man talk."

"Since the movie is about the land, I'd like to start out there. Maybe on a horse, riding slowly, stopping at the ridge and looking down the valley. How do you think that would work?"

Shanda nodded. "Perfect. While the credits are showing, we could be following you in the background. Do you have any place in mind?"

He nodded. "We could take a ride out there after supper."

"Great. I was wondering about something else. The barbeque Sunday gave me the idea. You know the part about the barn raising? Do you suppose we could end the day with a party and get the square dancers in there?"

"What about music?" Barry asked.

"I called Felix," she said absently. "He's already at work on it. I'll have to let him know about the dance scene. But we'll probably just use something from that period."

"Who's going to do the graphics?"

"Andy Canelli."

"Good."

He directed his next question to J.B. "You know that we're going to need a couple of VCRs to edit the videotape, don't you?"

"Don't know a thing about it," J.B. said imperturbably. "Just tell me what you need and I'll send for it. Or, better yet, you can go into town and pick it out yourself."

The three of them sat planning the next few days until Ruby came out muttering about good food going cold and shepherded them inside.

"Aunt Paige! How are you?" During the next week, each time Shanda heard the telephone ring she was sure it was Jake, finally calling to vent his anger. So she was grateful to hear her aunt's astringent tone. "Did you get the copies of the family charts I sent you?"

"That's why I'm calling." Paige sounded peeved. "Are you sure they're accurate?"

"Absolutely. These ladies spent an entire day with me, explaining the intricacies of the family lines. They were born and raised here, and what one didn't know, three others could document. What makes it so confusing, of course, is that four of Buell's brothers followed him and settled in the town. Every time you turn around, you're bumping into a McCade."

"But none of them are direct descendants of Buell?"

"No. Just as the obituary stated, J.B. was his only child."

"Of his second marriage," Paige reminded her.

"Right. And the line dies there because J.B.'s son is adopted." Shanda spoke quickly, hoping to divert her aunt from the subject of Buell's divorce. The longer she stayed at the ranch, the fonder she became of J.B. and the more apprehensive she became about the outcome of her search for evidence of that divorce.

If Buell hadn't had the sense to end his marriage to that toothless old lady legally—of course, she was probably young and pretty when they married because, if the gossip of the older ladies was to be believed, that was the only type he was ever attracted to—then J.B. could be in for big trouble. Shanda had nightmares of unscrupulous relatives—half relatives, she corrected herself—popping out of the woodwork and initiating lawsuits to claim part of J.B.'s fortune. God knows, she thought gloomily, there are enough people in the world like that. One of them could certainly be somewhere in the family.

If the town ladies were to be believed, J.B. was fortunate not to have been involved in such a suit already. Buell had been a handsome rascal who had an eye for women. He was considered an eligible bachelor and lived accordingly. He once had a transfer business which kept him on the move, and gossip had it that the McCade blue eyes could be found in more than one small town in his territory. Who knows, the ladies had questioned with laughter, how many of Buellton's early blue-eyed citizens were born on the wrong side of the blanket?

Scandalous speculation was one thing, Shanda decided. Probably, every town, large or small, had their share of it. But she didn't want to be the one to find hard evidence that would cloud the name of Buellton's founder.

"What did you say?" Shanda asked, not believing she had heard her aunt correctly.

"I said you don't have to bother about Buell's divorce. I found out."

"How? When?"

"It's a long story, but very interesting," Paige began, obviously settling down for a blow-by-blow description of the event.

"This is a long-distance call," Shanda reminded her.

"I'll take the short version."

"My grandmother, Buell's first wife," Paige began concisely, "had a sister Maude. Maude kept a journal. You know how common it was for people of that generation to keep them."

"Uh-huh," Shanda encouraged.

"Especially the ones who had any sort of an education."

"Uh-huh."

"You know how invaluable journals are in my research, of course—"

"I know, Aunt Paige. I *know*. What did she say?"

"When Maude died," Paige continued in a measured tone while Shanda groaned silently, "she left her journal to her daughter. Her daughter had no children of her own and the book ended up in the hands of her stepson, my contemporary. Can you believe it, Shanda? All these years I have periodically sent out letters to family members reminding them of my interest in the McCade history and this nincompoop finally remembers Maude's journal. Can you believe it?"

"I believe it," Shanda said, convinced that Paige would continue drifting off on byways and never finish. "What did *he* say?"

"He said he just remembered the journal, and since it really had nothing to do with his family, he thought I might be interested in having it. Of course, I called him and told him I was."

"Of course," Shanda said in resignation, wondering what the long version was like. "And then?"

"He mailed it to me. I received it last week. It's been no small task deciphering it. The woman had abominable handwriting."

"Aunt Paige," Shanda enunciated clearly, "what did Maude have to say about your grandmother?"

"She said Lily, my grandmother, was a pretty featherhead and got no better than she deserved. Sounds jealous to me."

"No doubt. Go on," Shanda urged, "then what?"

"She said Lily put her foot down when Buell wanted to leave Kentucky and go to Oklahoma. She had two children and another one on the way and wasn't about to travel in that condition. Buell agreed that they should wait until the child was born. He worked at all sorts of extra jobs to earn money for the trip. When the baby was born, Lily told him she wasn't going. She didn't want to leave her family and friends. Maude said that Lily was spoiled and expected Buell to 'knuckle under.' He didn't.''

''What happened?''

''Maude was living with them to help with the baby, and that's how she knew all about it. Her sympathies were apparently with Buell. She said the marriage had been a mistake from the beginning and they all knew it. He issued an ultimatum. He was going—with or without Lily. It was her choice, but he warned her that he wouldn't be back.''

Shanda's ear was glued to the receiver. ''What did she do?''

''Lily told Buell to go if he had to, but she knew he'd come back. Maude said she was a fool. I have the feeling Maude would have hiked up her skirt and trotted beside his horse if he had asked *her*. Anyway, he told Lily again that he wouldn't return. When she said she was staying, he gave her everything he had, keeping only his horse and enough money for some provisions; then he left.''

''Aunt Paige,'' Shanda asked in a feeble voice, ''did they get divorced?''

''Oh, that. Yes, they did.''

Just like that, Shanda thought in disbelief. She tosses it off with an ''oh, that,'' as if she had never been concerned about it. Then she realized that Paige had *not* been concerned, merely intrigued by the mystery. It would have added a bit of color to her book, but it really hadn't mattered one way or another.

Shanda fumed silently, remembering the days she had spent ruining her eyes reading microfilmed records of old newspapers and the hours spent sitting on hard benches at the Bureau of Vital Statistics waiting in vain for information. She had been developing an ulcer over the whole thing for nothing!

"Don't you want to hear the rest?" Paige asked, puzzled at Shanda's silence.

"I don't want to miss a word. You can even go on to the long version if you want to." Aunt Paige would never change. She would always be on to the next story, the next mystery. And, someday, Shanda would once again be snookered into doing something she didn't want to do, merely because Aunt Paige asked it of her. Things were back to normal. Thank God!

"Well, Maude stayed with Lily for the next couple of years. Lily told everyone in town that Buell had gone off to a good job and would be back. After a while, people just quit asking about him. She received a couple of papers from a lawyer and she tore them up. Then one day an official decree of divorce arrived. Lily read it and burned it. She spent the rest of her life pretending that Buell would be back. He sent money to her until the children were grown."

"The woman was a fool," Shanda said. "From what I've learned about him, he was quite a man."

"That seemed to be Maude's opinion, too," Paige agreed. "By the way, when I asked you to get me a scoundrel, I didn't really expect you to send one."

"What are you talking about?" Shanda asked blankly.

"Who, not what. That black-eyed devil you sent out to see me."

"Jake? Jake's been out there?"

"That he has."

"When?"

"A few days ago."

"Did he cause any trouble?" He still didn't believe her! He actually went out to check up on her!

"That all depends on your point of view." Paige sounded amused.

"What do you mean?"

"When he got here, I was trying to get them to release me from the hospital. No one was paying attention to me and I was furious."

"Did he stay and talk to you?"

"No, he listened. Then he acted. Within two hours he had me home and had arranged for a nurse to be with me as long as I needed her. He was out here for a couple of days. I saw quite a bit of him. He was delightful, even if a bit autocratic."

"That he is, autocratic, I mean. What on earth did you find to talk about?" Shanda asked uneasily.

"You, for the most part."

"I hope you didn't tell him anything."

"What's there to hide? I'm very proud of you. It does seem sudden, though."

"I've lost you. What does?"

"I know a man like that makes thinking difficult, but have you really considered it carefully?"

Shanda stared at the ceiling. Following Paige's conversational hairpin turns was difficult at the best of times, but right now it was impossible. What in heaven's name was she talking about?

"Have I considered what carefully?" she asked with all the patience she could muster.

"Taking a step like that, of course." Her aunt's tone expressed surprise.

"Like what, Aunt Paige?" she asked through gritted teeth.

"Don't be dense, Shanda. Surely it's no secret?"

While Shanda pondered her aunt's last comment, she heard a medley of voices raised in greeting. Aunt Paige had company and that meant that this puzzling exchange would be terminated in the next thirty seconds.

"I have visitors, Shanda. I'll talk with you soon. Good-bye, dear."

"Wait a minute, Aunt Paige!" Shanda shouted. "What's no secret?"

"Why, your marriage. Jake said he was going to marry you."

Shanda lowered the receiver and stared at it as if it were an oracle about to speak. Instead, it merely buzzed a dial tone at her. Dropping it into place, she rolled to the side of the bed and sat up. Marry Jake? Her heart thumped erratically at the thought. Why would he tell Aunt Paige that? she wondered in bewilderment. Of course. A cynical expression crossed her face. Jake would recognize that Paige was a lady of propriety. Even he would hesitate to inform her that his intentions were to bed her niece as quickly as he could manage it.

But he had gone too far this time. Her aunt had probably already called her parents and the news would be spreading through the family network. Of course, it didn't seem to matter to him.

She prowled up and down the room like a restless cat. He would rue the day he had heard of Shanda St. James. She didn't know exactly what she'd do, but she had always been fairly inventive. She was concentrating when J.B. knocked on her door.

"Shanda? You've got a visitor."

"Who is it?" she asked, opening the door.

"I'm not sure," he said, subduing a grin. "He seems to think we all know him." His lips twitched in amusement. "I think it's the Rhinestone Cowboy."

Chapter Ten

Shanda burst into the den with J.B. at her heels. "Lee! What on earth are you doing here?"

"Hi, darling." Lee slid an arm around her waist and kissed her lightly on the lips. "I finally remembered his name. All the way to New York I kept thinking about it. McBain, McClaine, McKane. None of them sounded right. You should have left me a note at the hotel," he chided. "I would have been here that next day. As it was, once I got to the Big Apple, I had to stay with my manager for a couple of weeks."

Shanda edged out of his embrace, aware of J.B.'s inquisitive look. She smoothed back an errant strand of hair and said, "Lee, this is Jake's father, J. B. McCade. J.B., Lee Masters." She watched as the men shook hands and noted that J.B.'s fascinated gaze never left the younger man.

It was understandable. Lee had dressed for the occasion. He had on new lizard-skin cowboy boots, designer jeans and an iridescent Western shirt that flashed from purple to pink to blue. It also had yards of embroidery work in loops and scrolls and was embedded with a few scattered sparkling stones. The outfit was topped off by a buff-colored Stetson that added inches to his large frame.

"When I got back to Oklahoma City, I called the house and learned that you were here at a ranch," Lee said, looking at Shanda. "I wanted to see you right away, but I stopped and did some shopping first," he continued, indicating his clothes.

"What store did you go to?" J.B. asked with interest.

With a quelling glance, Shanda interrupted. "Where are you staying?"

"I don't know. I drove right here. I didn't realize it would be so far away from everything."

"You're welcome to stay here," J.B. said heartily. "We've got plenty of room. Bring in your stuff and make yourself at home."

"Now we'll never get rid of him, J.B.," Shanda wailed as the front screen door slammed behind Lee. "Why on earth did you do that?"

"Just plain old Southern hospitality," he murmured. "Besides, I want to see what else he has in his suitcase."

"You're a miserable, rotten man," she declared, laughing despite her exasperation. "And complicating my life terribly."

"Just adding a bit of spice, honey."

"Shanda," Barry called as he trotted down the stairs reading some scribbled notes on a pad. "Are we going to do the crowd scenes tomorrow? If we can get started early, I might get them all in. Then all we'll have to do is finish the last bit with J.B. and we'll be—Oh, my God," he finished in a tone of utter disgust as Lee walked through the door.

"Hi, Nolan." Lee looked up with a genial smile. "What did you do, ruin some film?"

Ruby's voice preceded her through the hall door. "Supper's going to be ready in a little while. I thought I heard someone come in. Should I set another plate—" Her pink cheeks grew rosier as she came to an abrupt halt, staring at the dazzling sight before her. Her reaction, Shanda noted, differed from J.B.'s. Ruby was not amused.

"What's the matter, Ruby?" J.B. asked his open-mouthed cook in concern. "Aren't you feeling well?"

Barry rolled his eyes and groaned.

"Lee Masters! In our home! Well, I never—Do you want some coffee? Have a seat." A flustered Ruby rubbed her hands on her apron and dragged Lee to a large, comfortable chair. "Sit, sit," she urged. "Cream in your coffee? Sugar?" She rushed out of the room and they could hear silverware hitting the floor and dishes clattering.

"What in tarnation is the matter with her?" J.B. muttered to Shanda as Ruby zipped back into the room to deliver the coffee, then missed the door and bumped into the wall as she backed out of the room. Lee sipped his coffee with the calmness of a man accustomed to drinking in the midst of chaos.

At dinner, Shanda watched as J.B.'s bewilderment grew in direct proportion to Barry's disgust. Ruby flew back and forth, her ample bosom heaving with her exertions. Lee rewarded her nonstop service with a flashing smile, which momentarily stopped her in her tracks.

Once Ruby was occupied with washing the dishes and the dining room was quiet, Lee swirled the wine in his glass and asked Barry, "What are you doing here?"

"Just shooting some stuff for Shanda," he answered vaguely.

"What kind of stuff?"

"They're making a movie for me," J.B. said. "About the old days in Buellton."

Lee snapped to attention, staring at the older man. "A Western?"

"Not really," Shanda said hastily.

"Well, you might call it that," J.B. said in the same breath.

"I've always wanted to do a Western," Lee said, watching J.B. like a dog eyeing a bone.

"You know Shanda only does documentaries," Barry said, nudging J.B.'s foot.

J.B. looked at Shanda in confusion. "This isn't a documentary, is it?"

"They won't let me do a Western," Lee complained.

"This isn't your sort of thing at all," Shanda told Lee. "It's not a regular movie. There's not enough scope for you."

"Who won't?" J.B. asked.

"My agent. I always have to be a pirate."

"Because you're a *good* one. Isn't he, Barry?" Shanda kicked her friend beneath the table.

"Terrific," he said, wincing.

"I could be an even better cowboy, but they won't let me try."

"I think it's a damned shame he has to be a pirate if he doesn't want to be," J.B. said, enjoying himself immensely.

"He really loves it," Shanda assured him. "Don't you, Lee?"

"It's not bad, I guess. I just want to try being a cowboy."

"You're doing the crowd scenes tomorrow, aren't you?" J.B. asked Shanda. She nodded, then stopped midway, almost giving herself whiplash, as she caught his train of thought. He turned back to Lee. "Why don't you come out to Old Town tomorrow and join the cast? I've got a horse you can ride," he continued, ignoring his companions' stricken expressions.

Lee brightened. "I'm a quick study," he promised J.B. before turning to Shanda. "Where's my script?"

"No script. No lines," she said in a tone meant to discourage him.

Lee shook his head dubiously. If there was one thing he understood, it was the market. "There's not much interest in silent films these days," he informed Shanda. Once that bit of information had been passed on, he sat quietly, lost in thought.

J.B. took refuge behind his cup of coffee, escaping the dark looks coming at him from two pair of eyes.

"What color?" Lee came back to life and directed his question at J.B.

"Huh?" J.B.'s glance shifted to Shanda and saw that she looked as confused as he felt.

"The horse, what color is it? My other outfit is brown," he explained, assuming they would grasp the significance. "A palomino would look nice. Or a white one."

"Aw, too bad," Barry said hastily, "all his horses are

brown. Dark brown.'' At J.B.'s look of utter astonishment, he covered his face with his napkin, coughing and gasping.

"I've got some beige pants," Lee announced. "Designer, of course. I must have something that'll go with them." He rose, abstracted. "I'll be back in a few minutes."

J.B. broke the silence. "Where in the holy hell did he come from?"

"Hollywood," Shanda gurgled.

"Oh." His tone indicated that that explained everything.

"You still don't know who he is, do you?" Father and son had a lot in common, she thought, as she once again explained that Lee was the star of "Nemesis."

"You mean the one that prances around in—"

"Yes!" she interrupted before Barry could latch on to the descriptive phrase.

"Had to buy Ruby her own TV so I could get some peace on Monday nights," he grumbled.

Barry withdrew his face from his napkin. "He wants to mix and match his horse and pants," he said in a quavering voice. The three of them made such a commotion that Ruby stuck her head through the swinging door to see what she was missing.

The next day at Old Town was as bad as they suspected it would be. The volunteers from town had arrived promptly, and Shanda was using a bullhorn to explain in which order the various scenes would be shot when J.B. and Lee rode over the crest of the hill. A ripple of feminine whispers, sounding like leaves rustling in a breeze, was the first indication that Lee had arrived. The next was a mass exodus.

As Lee swung down from his horse, he was surrounded by a cross section of his Monday evening following—from lithe, tan teenagers to a flushed octogenarian. They pressed against him, requesting autographs and pictures.

Giving in to the inevitable, Shanda mentally rearranged the schedule and told Barry that they would begin with the barn-raising scene, which called for only the men. She walked over to J.B. "It looks as though your Southern hospitality is going to set us back two or three days."

J.B. grinned, watching the milling throng before him. "It's worth it. Anyway, you said you were ahead of schedule." Looking down at her, he remarked casually, "Jake called before we left the house. Lee answered." At her wince, he said, "Lee said that you two were engaged. Sounded like he had mentioned it to Jake before. By the time I got to the phone, they were both pretty hot under the collar."

"Damn!"

"Are you?"

"Engaged? No. At least not anymore. But Lee's . . . tenacious. Once he gets an idea into his head, it's hard to change it. What did Jake have to say?"

"He'll be home sometime tomorrow evening." Her heart jumped and her blood raced and she almost missed his next words. "By the way, I told him what you're doing for me."

"I thought he wasn't supposed to know," she said, startled.

"He wasn't. But that was only at first, so he wouldn't interfere. Frankly, I didn't think my friends could keep him out of my hair this long, so it went better than I expected."

Her eyes shone with laughter. "Do you mean that those

men have been skipping around the country playing hide and seek with Jake?''

''Yep.'' His deep chuckle blended with her giggle. ''But don't tell him or I'll never get him to do me a favor again.''

''You mean he doesn't know?''

He patted her on the shoulder. ''Suspecting's one thing; knowing's another.''

By working straight through the day and ruthlessly ordering J.B. to distract Lee, they finished just as the sun slid behind the hills. Barry looked up from packing his equipment away, glowering at Lee's retreating form. ''If he had ruined one more scene by looking up and flashing his Chiclet teeth at the camera, I was going to cream him.''

''Thank God that part's over,'' she agreed wearily. ''We'll lock ourselves in the workroom tonight and edit today's footage. J.B. can baby-sit his guest.

The staccato rap of a Ping-Pong ball on a table resurrected from J.B.'s basement and used for a series of wild, round robin tournaments stopped abruptly. It was followed by an assortment of groans and a triumphant, ''Wahoo! The winner and still champ, Shanda St. James!''

She was in the midst of a solitary victory dance, whirling around the screened back porch when she slipped. Before she could even cry out, she was caught and swung against a warm, muscular frame. Jake! She didn't question the instinctive knowledge. It was enough that her body rejoiced at the contact.

She looked up, beyond shirt buttons and Adam's apple, chin and firm lips, to dark eyes that branded her with a possessive, searing expression. It was that look which brought her back to her senses and replaced her dazed expression with one of determination. Backing away was a lost cause—his arms had locked around her waist and showed no signs of relaxing—but she wedged her hands between them and pushed against his chest.

It was like trying to move a rock, she decided. She blew back a strand of hair that had fallen across her brow and said, "I want to talk to you."

"It's about time," he muttered, lowering his face.

He obviously had more than talk on his mind, but she wasn't about to provide a show for the three men who had fallen into a fascinated silence.

"Don't you dare—" she breathed as he cupped her hips, lifted her and turned so that his back was to the room. Too late, she thought, as his warm lips covered hers. I'm always too—Seconds, minutes or hours later, he lifted his head, holding her in the protective arch of his body as tiny tremors shivered through her.

"Let's go out to dinner," he murmured against her ear. "We don't need an audience tonight." He waited until she nodded in agreement before he released her. "Go get dressed," he suggested. "Meet you back down here in an hour."

Shanda backed through the door, grateful that his bulk protected her from the curious looks of the others. Dashing up the stairs, the strength returning to her limbs as the distance between them increased, she thought about her reaction to him, to his kisses. "Got to do something about that," she muttered.

Half an hour later, she stepped out of the shower and blew her hair dry, still wondering. What do you do when your brain is flashing a red alarm and your body is panting

"Yeah, yeah!" Slipping into panties and bra, she muttered in disgust, "So far, the ayes seem to have it!"

She poked a button on her tape recorder and J.B.'s voice flowed through the room. While she listened to him, she opened the closet door and looked over her dresses. Lately, she had little time to hear the cassettes J.B. made for Paige. Not wanting to miss anything, she kept one in the recorder at all times. Putting back a crimson-suede dress with flowing Cossack sleeves, she laughed aloud at J.B.'s comment about a business rival. He was in rare form on this one! With each cassette, he seemed more comfortable and less restrained.

She had, she realized, taken out and returned every single garment in the closet. Finally she grabbed her what-to-wear-when-all-else-fails dress and slipped into it. "It" was a sleeveless wisp of black with a V neck and back and narrow shoulders. She had decided long ago that the neck was low enough to stir interest, but not so low that it would elevate her date's blood pressure. Quickly, she added black sling-back pumps, a bracelet and a spray of perfume, grabbed a matching stole and shut off the recorder. Then she started down the stairs.

Jake stood at the bottom, waiting for her. When she saw him she stopped as if she had run into a wall, wanting nothing more than to turn and bolt. The gleam in his eyes warned her that he was already on simmer, rapidly rising to flash point.

He bundled her into the car—a large one with bench seats, she noted absently—and maneuvered it smoothly down the driveway. He held out his hand until she reluctantly put hers into it. "Come over and join me," he invited. He waited until she edged over, then he put her hand on his warm thigh, with his firmly on top of hers, keeping it in place. "That's better. Now, tell me what he's doing here."

"Lee," she acknowledged with a sigh. "I think he was bored. When he left New York, he decided to come back here and look me up."

Jake's sideways glance was cynical, then slowly became thoughtful. She really believed it. He looked down at her, his gaze following the neckline of her dress to the fascinating display of curves. She didn't realize that she was so damned sexy she'd have men bumping into each other wherever she went. Or traveling across the country. Or whatever else it took.

"Then he decided that he wanted to be a cowboy," she continued, straight-faced.

"So?"

"But his pants didn't match any of the horses."

"*What?*"

"J.B. was absolutely fascinated. He followed Lee around for an hour while he held up first one outfit and then another to all the horses." Her eyes were brimming with humor as she met his disbelieving gaze. She nodded solemnly, crossing her heart, and watched his lips curve into a reluctant grin. "When J.B.'s men saw what he was up to, they invited him out to the bunkhouse for a poker game."

"How did he do?"

"He's three hundred ahead so far."

Jake's laugh was a deep rumble, lifting her up and carrying her along until they were both teary-eyed and weak. "Tell me all about it," he demanded. "Don't leave out a thing."

The long drive seemed short as Shanda recounted Ruby's reaction, J.B.'s disbelief, the charging women and Barry's curses. They arrived at the steakhouse limp with laughter and with Shanda's body pressed comfortably against his.

"You'll like this place," Jake said into the sudden stillness of the car. "It's reasonably quiet, the food's great and it's just dark enough."

Shanda touched his arm. "Just a minute, Jake. Before we go in, I want to ask you something." Their faces were illuminated by the headlights of a passing car. "It's about what you said to Aunt Paige."

"I wondered when you'd get around to that," he remarked casually.

"You really told her we were getting married!" she said in disbelief.

"To be absolutely accurate, I told her I was going to marry you."

"I may be thick, but I fail to see the difference."

He turned to face her, sliding his arm along the seat behind her. She got her usual sense of claustrophobia as he seemed to surround her. He just *loomed* so.

"Don't get on your high horse now. Give me a minute and I'll explain. While I was gone, I decided that the only way we could make this thing between us work would be to get married. But since I hadn't mentioned it to you yet, I couldn't honestly tell your aunt you were going to marry me."

"That's great. Just great. I suppose you know that by now my mother's got the telephone glued to her ear telling every one of my relatives the good news." Infuriated by the soft gust of laughter in her ear, she thumped him on the shoulder with a small fist and stormed, "Don't make fun of me, Jake. I'm mad. From that first evening in the hotel, you've made no secret of the fact that you want me in your bed. Hanging a pretty name on it doesn't change anything.''

''Wrong, honey. It changes everything. What went on before was chasing.''

''And?'' She wished her challenge didn't sound quite so breathless.

He traced a warm finger down the V of her dress to its extreme point and smiled as he felt the crazy drumming of her heart. His hand cupped the warm, full curve of one breast, then it moved to lift her chin up. Positioning her face so that her lips were just beneath his, he murmured, ''This is courting.''

His lips brushed hers once, soft and tantalizing, before they settled down to serious business. He was doing it again, she realized hazily—knocking down her defenses, claiming her, making her admit that she was a woman with needs and desires that only he could fulfill. She moaned as his hand slipped back down, stroking, caressing. He lifted his head, then bent once again to touch her lips with a whisper of a kiss.

She touched her tender lips with shaking fingers. ''Why do you do this to me?'' she asked shakily. ''Why don't you just leave me alone?''

His answer was simple. ''I can't. I need you. *You*, not any other woman in the world.''

Dropping her head back on his shoulder, she whispered, ''You're going too fast for me. I don't know anything about you. All I know is that you drive me crazy and that you kiss like an angel. Or a devil,'' she finished and felt a quiver of amusement run through him.

''Come inside with me,'' he coaxed, trying not to laugh. ''I'm going to feed you, build up your strength, and then tell you everything you want to know. That's what tonight is all about. Once you learn how lovable I am, you won't have the heart to turn me down.''

And that apparently was the program for the evening. He talked through the heaping salads they built at the salad bar, telling her what it was like growing up on the ranch with Jenny and J.B. in a house filled with laughter and love. She watched his face grow somber as he talked of darker days.

''Then, when I was thirteen, Jenny died. It was as if our part of the world died with her. J.B. seemed to grow old overnight. No matter how many windows I opened or how many curtains I pulled back, the house was dark. I was scared to death that J.B. was going to die, too.'' Shanda touched his hand, wanting to comfort that young boy whose pain still lurked in the eyes of the man next to her.

Jake laced his fingers through hers and sat quietly for a while. ''J.B. couldn't stay at the ranch. He bought the house in Oklahoma City and decided to get more involved in the business end of things. He doubled his assets the first year. The next year, he did it again. He dealt fairly with everyone, but he also knew how to go straight for the jugular when the occasion called for it.''

He leaned back while their dishes were removed. ''When I wasn't in school, I was with him. I watched and I learned. And I took care of him.'' He smiled wryly. ''Or at least I thought I did. He was smart enough to know that I needed to be needed.''

Shanda didn't move, her fingers still entwined warmly in his. She blinked back tears, thinking of the two of them exorcising their pain with work as they reinforced the bond between them. Built it into a chain with no weak links.

A waiter slipped steaks the size of platters in front of

them, effectively breaking the poignant mood. "So I went to college," Jake continued at her expectant look, "and got a degree in business administration. J.B. turned a lot of stuff over to me and started spending more time at the ranch. He mellowed and I became the shark." His smile was a white slash in his dark face.

"And you never married." It was a statement, not a question.

"No. At first I told myself that no one was ever going to mean so much to me that I could be hurt the way J.B. was when Jenny died. Later I knew I wasn't being very realistic, but I never met anyone I wanted to marry. Until now."

"Talk about being realistic!" Shanda said nervously. "We only met a month ago, and we've spent more hours talking on the phone than we have in each other's company. It's too soon, Jake."

"The first time J.B. saw Jenny, he knew she was the one for him. They were married within a week."

"The first time you saw me," she returned with spirit, "you were convinced that I was up to no good. And I don't know that your opinion has ever changed."

They were still arguing as they drove up to the house.

"I've waited this long," Shanda said for the tenth time, "and I'm not going to rush into something that could cause us both a lot of grief."

"Why can't you listen to reason?" he asked in exasperation as he slammed the front door.

Reason! she thought in a fine fury as she trotted up the stairs with him right behind her. Reason? Because he'd given her every one except the one she wanted to hear. Not one word about love! He wanted her, was determined to have her, etc., etc., etc. She desperately needed to hear him say "I love you." Because when she saw him waiting at the foot of the stairs, she had known that he was the one she had been waiting for all of her life. Had known that her sleepless nights were caused by more than his midnight calls. Had known that when she drove her red car out of his life, she would be leaving behind the only man she could ever love. And he talked about reasons!

He slammed her bedroom door behind him and she turned on him angrily. "Wake up everybody in the house, why don't you!"

"At ten-thirty?" he asked in a level tone. "I doubt it." He took off his jacket and tossed it onto the back of the chair. His tie followed it. Walking toward her, he unfastened the first three buttons of his shirt and rolled his sleeves up a couple of turns. His voice was quiet. "Why are you so angry?"

She turned her back to him, not liking the way he was scrutinizing her. He had an analytical mind and she knew that unless he was distracted, he would be uncomfortably near the truth in a very short time. And she wasn't about to make herself any more vulnerable than she already was.

"I'm not angry, I'm upset."

"Why are you upset?"

"I don't know," she said, thinking frantically. The wretched man sounded as though he was prepared to spend the night playing twenty questions. "You've surprised me and I don't like being pressured."

"That doesn't make sense. With a job like yours, you deal with pressure all the time."

"Don't get logical when I'm being emotional," she flared, turning to face him.

"All right, we'll be emotional together." His smile

warned her, but not soon enough. She backed away, but not soon enough.

"Jake, don't," she wailed softly. "I can't think when you do this!"

"That's the idea."

Twenty minutes later, curled up in his lap, she nodded groggily when he sighed and said, "All right, we'll talk about it tomorrow." Nodding at the recorder beside him on the table, he asked, "What kind of music is it?"

"Oh, that's just a tape J.B. made for Aunt Paige. Turn it on."

As he listened, shock jerked him erect and he swore softly. He turned the machine off and ejected the cassette. "There's enough on here to keep him in court answering libel cases the rest of his life. I want this cassette, Shanda."

Stunned by his reaction, she rolled off his lap and stood before him. "No."

"You don't understand—"

"Yes, I do," she said. "I understand that you don't trust me. That tape was made for me and you're talking about libel suits. I'm not planning to sell the information on it, Jake." She held out her hand. "You can't have it," she said deliberately.

After a silence that seemed to last forever, he dropped it into her hand, picked up his jacket and tie and left the room, closing the door behind him.

Chapter Eleven

If only he had slammed the blasted door, she thought crossly the next afternoon, she would have felt better. The soft click of the latch had haunted her all night. Not quite ready to face him, she deliberately skipped breakfast and checked each room before entering, only to learn from J.B. that Jake had taken off in one of the trucks early that morning.

What was the matter with him? Granted, he was accustomed to watching over J.B. He had spent most of his life doing just that. But if he really wanted to marry her, was it asking too much to expect him to trust her? How on earth could he believe that she'd do anything to harm J.B.?

"I'm ready to go," Barry called, bringing her back to the present with a start. They were back on the ridge overlooking Old Town to do the final scene with J.B.

Normally, the first and last scenes would have been done at the same time because they were in the same location. Shanda shook her head, remembering how hastily the whole thing had been thrown together. Nothing was normal about this film.

"Okay, J.B." She turned to the older man with an affectionate smile. "Let's go over it one more time. Barry will open with a long shot. When he gets here"—she pointed—"you begin." J.B. nodded amiably and moved into position.

Two hours later they were finished. And none too soon, Shanda thought, watching a truck race toward them, spewing dust and gravel as it ground to a halt. Barry leaped to cover his camera as Jake strode toward them. He was still mad. Not just mad, she decided, *furious*.

If he had had any doubts, one encompassing glance cancelled them. The three of them and the camera told it all. His rage, as he turned to Shanda, left her shaken. "You finally got what you came for, didn't you?" His words came softly from between hard, stiff lips.

She looked bewildered even as she stiffened at his insulting tone.

"You do that innocent routine so well, I actually believed you. Congratulations, sweetheart, you conned the pro." His cold eyes measured her length. "What was the deal? A film for an interview? Along with those tapes, you should be set up for life."

Shanda stared back proudly, lifting her chin, waiting silently for him to finish.

"Just a damn minute, McCade. Who do you think you're talking to?" Barry's voice was cutting.

Shanda's outflung arm stopped him in his tracks as Jake

warned, "Back off, Nolan." Frozen with anger, Shanda waited for Jake to finish.

"Get your satisfaction from the filming of it," he said, each word falling like a chip of ice, "because you'll sure as hell not get off the ranch with it." He swung on his heel, almost ripped the door off its hinges as he got into the truck and tore back down the road.

Shanda stared after him until the truck was obscured by churning dust, then turned to J.B. "I thought you told him what we were doing."

"I did." He tilted back his Stetson thoughtfully, then continued. "But I forgot to tell him I was in it." He looked down at her proud, angry face and wanted to shake his stiffnecked son until his teeth rattled. "I'm sorry, honey."

"No need for you to apologize," she said quietly, sliding her trembling fingers into the back pockets of her jeans.

"He'll cool down in a little while."

"He may do that," she agreed tightly. "But I won't."

J.B. stared in consternation at the cold fury in her voice.

"Barry"—she turned to the silent man—"now that we've wrapped this up, you can finish, can't you?" At his nod, she said, "Good. Will you fly back, work with Felix and Andy on the music and graphics and then bring the film back to J.B.?"

"You know I will," he said soberly. "Where are you going to be?"

"I don't know," she replied with a frozen calm. "Anywhere but here."

The ride back was silent except for J.B.'s quietly voiced

question. "Won't you think it over, honey? Give it a little time?"

She placed her hand on his, squeezing tightly as she slowly shook her head from side to side.

Two hours later, she stood by the car in a crisp, gray linen pantsuit. Her composure cracked only when she turned to J.B. His concern was clear in his blue eyes so like her own. She stepped into his waiting arms, hugged him tightly, then stood on tiptoe to kiss his cheek. "Good-bye, J.B. Thanks for everything." She glanced fleetingly at the dress box he had tied and carefully placed behind the seat. Clearing her throat, she said, "I hope we can meet some time. Now that I've found you, I don't want to lose touch."

His face was set as he draped an arm around her shoulders. "What'll I tell Jake when he gets back?"

She stiffened, her voice hard. "Tell him the family silver is intact."

J.B. stood, hands on hips, watching until she was out of sight. "Jake, boy," he said aloud, "you're gonna have one helluva a time bringing that girl around. And you deserve every minute of misery she gives you." With that, he stomped up the stairs, slammed the door and poured himself a drink.

For a while Shanda drove blindly, just following the yellow line in the center of the road. Not once did she glance at the green rolling hills and neat white fences that made this part of the country look like something out of a child's picture book. When she reached I-35, she flipped a metal coin and while it was still in the air decided that she couldn't risk passing Jake on the way to Oklahoma City. She turned south, heading for Dallas or Fort Worth. She'd decide which when she had to. Right now the only thing that mattered was putting distance between herself and Jake.

Blinking, she finally allowed herself the release of tears. She groped in her purse for a tissue, grateful that she hadn't howled on J.B.'s chest. Although she had anticipated driving away and leaving him behind, somehow she hadn't visualized it as being so final. Or so painful. She and Jake could have built something beautiful together, she thought sadly. Something so bright and shining that it could light up a dark house for a little boy. Something like J.B. and Jenny had.

Realizing that her anger had dissolved into blubbering self-pity, she turned her thoughts to the furious man who had walked away from her. He could have asked, couldn't he? He could have trusted her enough at least to give her the benefit of the doubt. He could have done anything except just shoot accusations at her. Why in heaven's name did he ask her to marry him if he didn't trust her?

"You'll be sorry, Jake McCade!" she cried aloud. "You walked away from the best thing you'll ever find. My love! Me! I am one terrific person! And I have so much love to give to the right man, he won't even know what hit him!" Her voice cracked and she whispered, "And you, you stupid man, couldn't even see that you were the one."

She was so wrapped up in her misery that it took her a moment to realize that there was a police car behind her, its siren wailing and red light flashing. She glanced at the speedometer, wincing at the sight of the needle hovering at eighty-five. She slowed down gradually and pulled over to the side of the road. As she took another tissue from her purse, she checked the rearview mirror. A very large uniformed officer was approaching. She took one more swipe at her nose and rolled down the window.

"Traveling sort of fast, aren't you, ma'am?" he asked politely.

"Yes. I'm sorry." She looked at his tanned face and saw that he was taking in the ravages of her tears. "I was a little . . . upset, and didn't notice." At his request, she handed over her driver's license and rummaged through the glove compartment for the registration slip.

"California," he murmured, looking at her license. "Malibu. That's where all the movie stars live, isn't it?"

"Some," she said briefly. "I don't live in their part of town, though."

"Would you step out of the car, please?" He opened the door for her and waited.

She looked up in surprise, then moved slowly until she was standing before him. Wondering if he was going to ask her to walk an imaginary straight line beside the road, she regretted her high-heeled sandals.

"Would you open your trunk?" he asked.

Hesitating briefly, she said, "Oh, sure." After removing the keys from the ignition, she moved to the rear of the car and opened the trunk. "There," she said, stepping aside.

"This your luggage?"

"Of course." Who else's did he expect her to have?

"May I check the cases?" he asked in a formal tone.

"Check them?"

"Open them. Look through them," he spelled out patiently.

All this for a speeding ticket? she wondered. "There's nothing in there except my clothes." He remained at her side, waiting silently. She shrugged. "Be my guest." Her confusion mounted as he opened one bag, neatly shifted her clothes and ran his fingers over every square inch of the lining. He replaced her clothing, shaking and folding one garment at a time. The whole process was repeated with the second bag.

Flushing as he handled her panties and bras, she burst out, "What on earth are you looking for?"

"Drugs."

Her mouth fell open. "As in pot and cocaine?"

He nodded.

"I don't use that stuff!"

His gaze touched her face, once again noting her reddened eyes and nose.

"I've been *crying*," she said defensively.

"Um hmm."

Jamming her hands into her back pockets to keep them away from his throat, she paced back and forth as he examined the empty trunk with painstaking care. His partner, she noted, didn't seem excited about a possible drug bust. He was lounging on the passenger side, hat over his face, apparently taking a nap. She restrained herself until the officer reached inside for the box J.B. had tucked away with such loving care.

"Wait a minute!" She wrapped her arms around the box. "This needs to be handled very carefully."

"Um hmm." He could put more disbelief in a mumble than any man she knew, Shanda thought in disgust.

"It's a wedding dress. Very old and very fragile."

"Do *you* want to open it?"

"All right!" Carefully edging the twine over one corner, she slipped it down the sides of the box and eased off the cover. "See? A wedding dress."

"Will you take it out, please?"

Gritting her teeth at the polite request, Shanda lifted the dress and held it up while he felt through the folds of material. Perspiration was beginning to dot his forehead, she noted. Good! Maybe he'd have a heatstroke and she could get away while his partner snored in the car. "Satisfied?" she asked, after he made a thorough investigation of the box. He murmured something polite and ducked down to check the seats.

An hour later, Shanda was perched on the front fender of his car, eyeing him wrathfully as he squatted down to run his hand behind the grillwork of hers. Despite the fact that he was now frankly wiping sweat from his face with a handkerchief and checking his watch occasionally, he persevered. "The only thing that's left are my teeth," she commented icily. "Want to check them?"

Forty minutes later, she exploded. "Look, either give me a ticket for speeding and let me go or take me to the nearest town where I can talk to somebody who knows what he's doing! You've held me here for almost two hours on the flimsiest excuse I've ever heard of, and I've had it! Just because I'm from California and drive a flashy car doesn't mean I deal in drugs."

A large car shot by, pulled over to the side of the road with a tormented squeal of brakes and reversed noisily, raising a cloud of dust that showered the other two cars. Shanda scarcely noticed. "I've seen incompetence before, and I've seen stupidity before, but never have I seen such a stunning combination of the two! Unless you have some other hidden talents that you want to display, I demand that you let me go!"

For the first time, a grin crossed the face of the uniformed man. He turned to face her, looked over her shoulder and said, "You took your own sweet time getting here."

Jake, hitting the ground at a run, heard the last of Shanda's blistering tirade. He was too weak-kneed with relief to be amused. He had found her! Thank God. And now that he had, he realized, he didn't know where to start. How do you apologize for the unforgivable, for words that should never have been uttered? The only thing he was certain of was that neither of them would leave until the whole mess was straightened out. Until, God willing, she came back into his arms, her eyes shining with love.

Shanda turned and saw Jake loping toward her. Her eyes traveled from dusty boots and faded jeans to a blue, Western-style shirt fitting tautly over his shoulders. A quick glance at his face revealed a stubbornly set jaw and dark eyes full of relief and a host of other emotions that she couldn't begin to read. How could the sight of one man fill her with both joy and rage? she wondered.

"I owe you one, Jerry." Jake's deep voice was abrupt. "A *big* one. These last two hours seemed like ten." The two men exchanged a look over Shanda's head.

Jake nodded in agreement as he reached out to slam the Corvette trunk closed and remove the keys. Tossing them to Jerry, he asked, "Can you take this back to J.B.'s ranch for me?"

Shanda leaped for the keys, missed them by about a foot and found Jake's large hand wrapped around her wrist. "Just a minute!" she panted, tugging at her hand. "Those are *my* keys and that's *my* car. In case you haven't noticed, it's pointing *away* from J.B.'s ranch!"

"Move it out, Jerry."

"Don't you dare!" Shanda's voice was lost as the other man replied.

"You bet."

Jerry thumped a hand on the hood of his car, woke his sleeping partner and motioned for him to get behind the steering wheel. While Shanda stood restrained by Jake's hand, Jerry put her driver's license into her purse and placed it on the rear fender of Jake's car. He got into Shanda's Corvette, made a U turn and roared off.

"Let go of my wrist." Hearing the ice-coated words, Jake knew it was going to be tough sledding. But then he didn't deserve to have it made easy. Reluctantly dropping her hand, he vowed to give her the time and space she needed. He would take it slow and easy, build up her trust, let her know he wouldn't force her to do anything she didn't want to do.

He followed her as she picked up her purse and began walking. "Where are you going?"

"Dallas."

"It's a long way," he pointed out.

"It would have been shorter with my car," she said coolly.

He looked down at her impractical shoes. "You'll get blisters before you go a hundred yards."

"I'll have a ride before I get that far."

"The hell you will," he exploded, forgetting all his resolutions.

"Listen, Jake McCade," she flared. "You have no right to tell me what I will and won't do. You're not my keeper, you know."

"You need one," he roared, "if you think I'll let you get into a car with a strange man."

"So what's the big deal?" she shrieked. "I'm standing at the side of the road fighting with a strange man!"

"The big deal is," he said, suddenly quiet, "that you know I won't rape you."

She stopped, staring straight ahead. "You're right," she said, matching his stillness. "You may insult me or tear me to shreds, but you won't rape me." She drew in a ragged breath, clutching her purse to her stomach to quell a sudden surge of nausea. Still not looking at him, she asked, "What do you want, Jake?"

"Just to talk," he said softly. "Please?" His expression grew bleak as he watched her efforts to control the tears brimming in her eyes. She was so small, yet filled with quiet strength; so proud and so vulnerable. "Please," he urged.

"So talk," she said with disinterest. Anger filled him at her tone and he could have cheerfully throttled her.

"In the car," he said, reaching for her elbow.

Evading his hand, she turned and walked back to the car. "And then what?" she asked, stopping by the door.

"When we're through, if you still want me to, I'll take you back for your car." He opened the door, careful not to touch her.

"We'll stay here? You won't take me anywhere?" At his nod, she sat down, jumping as he slammed the door. He pulled the keys from his pocket and she eyed him nervously. Once he was behind the steering wheel, he dropped them in her lap.

"Insurance," he said casually. "We won't leave here until you give them back to me." She was plastered against the door, sitting as far as she could get from him, he noted grimly. In the long silence that followed, she eased her shoes off and curled up until her feet were resting on the seat, her knees under her chin, her arms wrapped around her legs. "First of all," he said, speaking to her profile, "I would like your forgiveness. I don't deserve it, but I need it."

She didn't move and he didn't know what to do next. It had all seemed so easy, he thought, fearful for the first time. He would find her, talk to her, convince her that he was a hopeless fool but worth forgiving, and they would live happily ever. But now that he had taken the first step, he wasn't so sure about the rest. She was so distant, so sheathed in ice that he didn't know how to reach her.

"If only you could understand how it's been with me and J.B.," he burst out. "I told you how he changed when Jenny died. Not with me, but in business dealings. He was ruthless. He made as many enemies as he did friends. By the time he handed things over to me, the pain was gone and he had reverted to his old, amiable, easy-going self. But he'll always be opinionated and outspoken. It's a bad combination when you're in his position. And times have changed. A lot of people don't settle their differences the way they used to, in a personal discussion. They do it in court. But as long as I'm around, he's not going to lose anything to a bunch of leeches in legal battles."

He shifted restlessly. "And then you came along. I practically fell down the stairs when I saw you. You were what I had been hunting for all my life, and you calmly took one look and said you didn't want me or anything I had." Shanda drew in an angry breath and wrapped her arms tighter around her legs.

"I made every wrong move I could possibly make where you were concerned. But, honey, I had no experience with love.'' She shot him a frankly disbelieving glance before returning to her sphinxlike position. "I said love," he emphasized. "I'm not repulsive and I'm rich. That's a turnon to a lot of women, so I've had my share and more of *experience*. But not with love.''

He gripped the steering wheel until his hands hurt. "I don't know what else to say except I'm sorry. I know I hurt you, Shanda. I can't forgive myself, but I need to hear you say that you can.''

Her face crumpled. "How could you think I'd do something to hurt J.B.? Couldn't you see how much I loved him? Couldn't you see how much I—'' Helplessly, he watched as sobs shook her. Afraid that she would bolt out of the door if he touched her, he eased closer, his face agonized as she pressed her face to her knees.

"When I saw you come down the stairs in that wedding dress and hold your hand out to J.B.," he whispered unsteadily, "I felt like someone was sticking a knife in my guts. I was jealous of my own father. I knew that I had to have you. And even if I lost you, the way he did Jenny, whatever time we'd had together would last me for a lifetime. So I went to see Paige and started my campaign with her.''

As her sobbing continued, he said roughly, "If you're going to break your heart, at least shed your tears on the one who caused them.'' He loosened the death grip she had on her legs and pulled her across his lap. His pounding heart almost stopped as she buried her face in the curve of his neck and wrapped one arm around his waist. Her other hand touched his cheek and froze as her thumb brushed across a wet path. Then her arm curved around his neck, nearly strangling him.

After a long silence punctuated only by sniffs and shuddering sighs, he simultaneously dared to breathe and to hope. "Shanda," he said tentatively, "do you forgive me?" She nodded and mumbled, "Yes," in a soggy voice.

"What did you mean when you said I should have known? Known what?"

"Nothing," she muttered.

"You should have known . . . that you loved me. You do, don't you, Shanda?" he asked anxiously.

"I do not," she denied swiftly.

He held her away from him, ordering, "Look me in the eye and tell me that." He watched her mutinous expression and for one terrified moment he thought she would.

"All right," she said belligerently. "I do. But why I do, I'll never know. You're arrogant and impossible and—" Her thoughts scattered in all directions as his arms wrapped around her, cutting off her breath. Then his lips covered hers and she gave up. Literally. For a lifetime.

Later, flushed and happy, once again resting her cheek against his shoulder, she said in a dreamy voice, "Jake, my work is important to me. Is that going to be a problem?"

"No. There are no problems that we can't handle. I know how much it means to you and I'm proud of the work you do. You've established a fine name and I want you to continue working under it."

She arched a brow. "You surprise me. You want me to keep my own name?"

"Only on film credits. And as long as the world knows that you're Jake McCade's woman."

"You're a possessive devil," she said placidly.

"Who kisses like an angel," he reminded her. "Now, if you'll promise to marry me, I'll tell J.B. that he can build us a storm cellar for a wedding present."

"I'll think about it," she promised with a grin.

"With a king-size bed," he added.

"Tempting," she admitted.

"And a Ping-Pong table. That's my last offer."

She looked up, brushing his lips with hers. "The things I'll do for a Ping-Pong table," she sighed.

Epilogue

Jake stretched and smiled, then reached out and drew Shanda's naked body close to his own. It was Saturday and they had nothing to do until that evening. Maybe they would stay in bed all day to celebrate. And then continue the celebration later on at J.B.'s. After all, they didn't have a second anniversary every day. It didn't seem possible that two years and four days ago they had been sitting in the car somewhere between Buellton and Dallas healing each other's wounds. Jake remembered how he had slid a sapphire ring on her finger, telling her it matched her eyes, and she had cried. He felt a surge of tenderness as he remembered.

"Jake," she had said softly, touching his cheeks with butterfly kisses until she reached his mouth. "Take me to your house."

"What for?" he asked blankly.

Slowly unbuttoning his shirt, she had smiled up at him. "I want to start filling in the gaps in my education." She ran her hand through the black mat of hair on his chest and looked at him expectantly. He kissed her hard, once, and dumped her unceremoniously on her side of the seat.

Buttoning his shirt, he said jerkily, "I'm not going to have my own father come after me with a shotgun." He rolled down the window and breathed deeply. "Where are the keys? We're getting out of here."

"For heaven's sake," she was still protesting as they approached the ranch, "I'm not a kid. I'm twenty-seven years old!"

He brought her hand to his mouth, placed a lingering kiss in its palm and gently closed her fingers over it. "And you've told me more than once that you've waited all this time. You can wait three more days."

It turned out to be four by the time J.B. brought a planeload of her family and friends from California. Four torturous days of watching her blue eyes fill with love and promise every time she looked at him. They were married at the ranch. Barry filmed the ceremony, but, even without pictures Jake would never forget it.

Shanda had glided down the stairs while he waited at the bottom. Smiling radiantly, she had held out a hand to him. He raised it to his mouth, kissed it softly, then tucked it securely in the curve of his arm. They had turned and walked to the front of the room together. He chuckled sleepily. It wasn't until he saw the film that he realized that damn cat had been at his side every step of the way.

He had gotten another wish fulfilled that day. Everyone in the English-speaking part of the world at least had learned that Shanda St. James was Jake McCade's woman. Because Lee was still there and some enterprising

photographer had taken a picture of him with the couple.
For once in his life, Jake thought, Lee had turned out to be
useful.

Three months ago, Shanda had received her Emmy. She
had been electrifying that night. He had been so proud of
her. He was just as proud of her now, he thought as he
gently caressed her, then rested his hand on her stomach.

Shanda chuckled, a soft sound against his shoulder.
"Feeling junior?" she inquired. "He's not going anywhere, my love. At least not for the next six months. Shall
we make an announcement tonight?" His soft murmur of
contentment as she wiggled closer could have meant
anything.

She grinned, remembering how she had tried to seduce
him. His resistance had lasted for four days and one hour
into the reception. They had left for his house, making
sure that Peg wasn't in the car with them. When she joined
him in the bedroom, she had dropped her negligee and
stood before him in a gown so sheer that her honey-gold
tan shone as if she were draped in raindrops.

"What's the matter, love?" she had whispered when he
made no move toward her.

His voice had been rough with emotion. "Shanda, I'm
so damned afraid I'm going to hurt you, I can't come any
closer."

"Jake, I'm not made of glass. I'm a woman. Your
woman." She moved until the tips of her breasts touched
his chest. "Feel me, Jake. Feel my love." Fortunately, he
had taken over at that point and she found that experience
was truly a wonderful thing.

He had been so proud when she won the Emmy. He had
insisted on building a special shelf in the bedroom for it.
"You earned it; you deserve to look at it." He had

grinned. "And since we spend more time in bed than anywhere else, this is where it goes."

"Jake," she said suddenly. "I've got an idea."

"I don't want to play Ping-Pong."

"Why not?"

"Because you always win."

"Well, that really wasn't what I was thinking about."

"And I don't want to leave this room."

"Why not?"

"Because that damn cat is stomping up and down the hall doing sentry duty, and he'll be right behind us as soon as we open the door."

She giggled, rubbing her cheek against his chest, enjoying the feel of his springy mat of hair. "I wasn't planning to leave the room."

"Oh?" One dark eye opened in interest.

"Or the bed."

He rolled over, caging her between his arms. "I'm yours to command," he said with a grin.

"Then love me, Jake."

His smile faded and his eyes were so tender, so vulnerable, she almost wept. "I do, baby, I do."

The soft sounds in the room were a testament to the fact that a shared experience is indeed a glorious thing.